SUPERNATURAL
KOREA

SUPERNATURAL
KOREA

MAGICAL TALES OF GOBLINS, DRAGONS, DEMONS AND MORE

STORIES BY

IM BANG, HOMER HULBERT AND OTHERS

ILLUSTRATED BY

MARCO FURLOTTI

TUTTLE Publishing

Tokyo | Rutland, Vermont | Singapore

Contents

Ten Thousand Devils

A certain Prince Han of Choong-cheong Province had a distant relative who was an uncouth countryman living in extreme poverty. This relative came to visit him from time to time. Han, pitying his cold and hungry condition, gave him clothes to wear and shared his food, urging him to stay and to prolong his visit often into several months. He felt sorry for him, but disliked his uncouthness and stupidity.

On one of these visits the poor relation suddenly announced his intention to return home, although the New Year's season was just at hand. Han urged him to remain, saying, "It would be better for you to be comfortably housed at my home, eating cake and soup and enjoying quiet sleep rather than riding through wind and weather at this season of the year."

He said at first that he would have to go, until his host so insistently urged him to stay that at last he yielded and gave consent. At New Year's Eve he remarked to Prince Han, "I am possessor of a peculiar kind of magic, by which I have under my control all manner of evil genii, and New Year is the season at which I call them up, run over their names, and inspect them. If I did not do so I should lose control altogether, and there would follow no end of trouble among mortals. It is a matter of no small moment, and that is why I wished to go. Since, however, you have detained me, I shall have to call them up in your Excellency's house and look them over. I hope you will not object."

Han was greatly astonished and alarmed, but gave his consent. The poor relation went on to say further, "This is an extremely important matter, and I would like to have for it your central guest hall."

Han consented to this also, so that night they washed the floors and scoured them clean. The relation also sat himself with all dignity facing the south, while Prince Han took up his station on the outside prepared to spy. Soon he saw a startling variety of demons crushing in at the door, horrible in appearance and awesome of manner. They lined up one after another, and still another, and another, till they filled the entire court, each bowing as he came before the master, who, at this point, drew out a book, opened it before him, and began calling off the names. Demon guards who stood by the threshold repeated the call and checked off the names just as they do in a government yamen. From the second watch it went on till the fifth of the morning. Han remarked, "It was indeed no lie when he told me 'ten thousand devils.'"

One latecomer arrived after the marking was over, and still another came climbing over the wall. The man ordered them to be arrested, and inquiry made of them under the paddle. The late arrival said, "I really have had a hard time of it of late to live, and so was obliged, in order to find anything, to inject smallpox into the home of a scholar who lives in Yong-nam. It is a long way off, and so I have arrived too late for the roll call, a serious fault indeed, I confess."

The one who climbed the wall, said, "I, too, have known want and hunger, and so had to insert a little typhus into the family of a gentleman who lives in Kyong-ki, but hearing that roll call was due I came helter-skelter, fearing lest I should arrive too late, and so climbed the wall, which was indeed a sin."

The man then, in a loud voice, berated them soundly, saying, "These devils have disobeyed my orders, caused disease and sinned grievously. Worse than everything, they have climbed the wall of a high official's house." He ordered a hundred blows to be given them with the paddle, the cangue to be put on, and to have them locked fast in prison. Then, calling the others to him, he said, "Do not spread disease! Do you understand?" Three times he ordered it and five times he repeated it. Then they were all dismissed. The crowd of devils lined off before him, taking their departure and crushing out through the gate with no end of noise and confusion. After a long time they had all disappeared.

Prince Han, looking on during this time, saw the man now seated alone in the hall. It was quiet, and all had vanished. The cocks crowed and morning came. Han was astonished beyond measure, and asked as to the law that governed such work as this. The poor relation said in reply, "When I was young I studied in a monastery in the mountains. In that monastery was an old priest who had a most peculiar countenance. A man feeble and ready to die, he seemed. All the priests made sport of him and treated him with contempt. I alone had pity on his age, and often gave him my food and always treated him kindly. One evening, when the moon was bright, the old priest said to me, 'There is a cave behind this monastery from which a beautiful view may be had; will you not come with me and share it?'

"I went with him, and when we crossed the ridge of the hills into the stillness of the night he drew a book from his breast and gave it to me, saying, 'I, who am old and ready to die, have here a great secret, which I have long wished to pass on to someone worthy. I have traveled over the wide length of Korea, and have never found the man till now I meet you, and my heart is satisfied, so please receive it.'

"I opened the book and found it a catalogue of devils, with magic writing interspersed, and an explanation of the laws that govern the spirit world. The old priest wrote out one magic recipe, and having set fire to it, countless devils at once assembled, at which I was greatly alarmed. He then sat with me and called over the names one after the other, and said to the devils, 'I am an old man now, am going away, and so am about to put you under the care of this young man; obey him and all will be well.'

"I already had the book, and so called them to me, read out the new orders, and dismissed them.

"The old priest and I returned to the temple and went to sleep. I awoke early next morning and went to call on him, but he was gone. Thus I came into possession of the magic art, and have possessed it for a score of years and more. What the world knows nothing of I have thus made known to your Excellency."

Han was astonished beyond measure, and asked, "May I not also come into possession of this wonderful gift?"

The man replied, "Your Excellency has great ability, and can do wonderful things; but the possessor of this craft must be one poor and despised, and of no account. For you, a minister, it would never do."

The next day he left suddenly, and returned no more. Han sent a servant with a message to him. The servant, with great difficulty, at last found him alone among a thousand mountain peaks, living in a little straw hut no bigger than a cockle shell. No neighbors were there, nor anyone beside. He called him, but he refused to come. He sent another messenger to invite him, but he had moved away and no trace of him was left.

Prince Han's children had heard this story from himself, and I, the writer, received it from them.

How Chin Outwitted the Devils

I n the good old days, before the skirts of Chosun were defiled by contact with the outer world or the "bird-twittering" voice of the foreigner was heard in the land, the "curfew tolled the knell of parting day" to some effect. There was a special set of police called *sul-la* whose business it was to see that no stray samples of male humanity were on the streets after the great bell had ceased its grumbling. Each of these watchmen was on duty every other night, but if on any night any one of them failed to "run in" a belated pedestrian it was counted to him for lack of constabulary zeal and he would be compelled to go on his beat the next night and every successive night until he did succeed in capturing a victim. Talk about police regulations! Here was a rule that, for pure knowledge of human nature put to shame anything that Solon and Draco could have concocted between them. Tell every policeman on the Bowery that he can't come off his beat till he has arrested some genuine offender and the Augean stables would be nothing to what they would accomplish in a week's time.

Such was the strenuous mission of Chin Ka-dong. One night it was his fate to suffer for his last night's failure to spot a victim. He prowled about like a cat till the "weesma' hours" and then, having failed to catch his mouse, ascended the upper story of the East Gate to find a place where he could take a nap. He looked over the parapet and there he saw, seated on the top of the outer wall which forms a sort of curtain for the gate, three hideous forms in the moonlight. They were not human, surely, but Chin, like all good policemen, was sans peur even if he was not sans reproche, and so he hailed the gruesome trio and demanded their business.

"We're straight from hell," said they, "and we are ordered to summon before his infernal majesty the soul of Plum Blossom, only daughter of Big Man Kim, of Schoolhouse Ward, Pagoda Place, third street to the right, second blind alley on the left two doors beyond the wine shop."

Then they hurried away on their mission, leaving Chin to digest their strange news. He was possessed of a strong desire to follow them and see what would happen. Sleep was out of the question, and he might run across a stray pedestrian, so he hurried up the street to Schoolhouse Ward, turned down Pagoda Place then up the third street to the right and into the second blind alley to the left and there he saw the basket on a bamboo pole which betokened the wine shop. Two doors beyond he stopped and listened at the gate. Something was going on within, surely, for the sound of anxious voices and hurrying feet were heard and presently a man came out and ran down the alley at a lively pace. Chin followed swiftly and soon had his hand on the man's collar.

"I'm afraid you're caught this time, my man. This is a late hour to be out."

"O, please let me go. I am after a doctor. The only daughter of my master is suddenly ill and everything depends on my haste."

"Come back," said Chin in an authoritative voice. "I know all about the case. The girl's name is Plum Blossom, and your master's name is Big Man Kim. The spirits have come to take her but I can thwart them if you come back quickly and get me into the house."

The man was speechless with amazement and fear at Chin's uncanny knowledge of the whole affair and he dared not disobey. Back they came, and the servant smuggled the policeman in by a side door. It was a desperate case. The girl was in extremis and the parents consented to let Chin in as a last chance.

On entering the room where the girl lay, he saw the three fiends ranged against the opposite wall, though none of the others could see them. They

winked at him in an exasperatingly familiar way and fingered the earthenware
bottles in their hands and intimated that they were waiting to take the girl's soul
to the nether regions in these receptacles. The moment had arrived and they
simultaneously drew the stoppers from their bottles and held them toward the
inanimate form on the bed.

But Chin was a man of action. His "billy" was out in an instant and with it
he struck a sweeping blow which smashed the three bottles to flinders and sent
them crashing into the corner. The fiends, with a howl, fled through a crack in
the window and left Chin alone with the dead—no, not dead, for the girl with
a sigh turned her head and fell into a healthful slumber.

It is hardly necessary to say that Chin was speedily promoted from *sul-la* to
the position of son-in-law to Big Man Kim.

But he had not heard the last of the devil's trio. They naturally thirsted for
revenge and bit their fingernails to the quick devising some especially exquisite
torment for him when they should have him in their clutches. The time came
when they could wait no longer and though the Book of Human Life showed

that his time had not come, they obtained permission to secure him if possible.

At the dead of night he awoke and saw their eyes gleaming at him through the darkness. He was unprepared for resistance and had to go with them. The way led through a desert country over a stony road. Chin kept his wits at work and finally opened a conversation with his captors.

"I suppose that you fiends never feel fear." "No," they answered, "nothing can frighten us," but they looked at each other as much as to say, "We might tell something if we would."

"But surely there must be something that you hold in dread. You are not supreme and if there is nothing that you fear it argues that you are lacking in intelligence."

Piqued at this dispraise, one of them said, "If I tell you, what difference will it make, anyway? We have you now securely. There are, in truth, only two things that we fear, namely the wood of the eum tree and the hair-like grass called *ki-mi-pul*. Now tell us what you in turn most dread."

"Well," answered Chin, "it may seem strange, but my greatest aversion is a big bowl of white rice, with kimchi and boiled pig on the side and a beaker of white beer at my elbow. These invariably conquer me." The fiends made a mental note.

And so they fared along toward the regions of the dead until they came to a field in which a eum tree was growing. The fiends crouched and hurried by but Chin by a single bound placed himself beneath its shade and there, to his delight, he found some of the hair-like grass growing. He snatched it up by handfuls and decorated his person with it before the fiends had recovered from their first astonishment.

They dared not approach and seize him, for he was protected by the tree and the grass, but after a hurried consultation two of them sped away on some errand while the other stayed to watch their prey. An hour later, back came the two, bearing a table loaded with the very things that Chin had named as being fatal to him. There was the white rice, the redolent kimchi, the succulent pig and the flagon of milk-white beer. The fiends came and placed these things as near as they dared and then retired to a safe distance to watch his undoing. Chin fell to and showed the power that these toothsome things had over him and when the fiends came to seize him he broke a limb off the tree and belabored them so that they fled screaming and disappeared over the horizon. So Chin's spirit went back to his body and he lived again. He had long been aware of some such danger and had warned his wife that if he should die or appear to die they should not touch his body for six days. So all was well.

Many years passed, during which Chin attained all the honors in the gift of his sovereign, and at last the time came for him to die in earnest. The same three imps came again, but very humbly. He laughed and said he was ready now to go. Again they traveled the long road but Chin was aware that they would try to steer him into Hell rather than let him attain to Heaven and he kept his eyes open.

One afternoon Chin forged ahead of his three conductors and came to a place where the road branched in three directions. One of the roads was rough, one smooth and on the other a woman sat beside a brook pounding clothes. He hailed her and asked which was the road to heaven. She said the smooth one, and before his guards came up, Chin was out of sight on the road to Elysium. He knew they would be after him, hot foot, so when he saw twelve men sitting beside the road with masks on their faces he joined them and asked if they did not have an extra mask. They produced one, and Chin, instead of taking his place at the end of the line, squeezed in about the middle and donned his mask. Presently along came the fiends in a great hurry. They suspected the trick that Chin had played but they saw it only in part, for they seized the end man and dragged him away to hell where they found they had the wrong man, and the judge had to apologize profusely for the gaucherie of the fiends.

Meanwhile the maskers were trying to decide what should be done with Chin. He was in the way and was creating trouble. They finally decided that as the great stone Buddha at Ung-chin in Korea was without a soul it would be a good thing to send Chin's spirit to inhabit that image. It was done, and Chin had rest.

Chin taught the Koreans one great lesson at least and that was that the devils are afraid of eum wood and the *ki-mi* grass, and since his time no sensible person will fail to have a stick of that wood and a bunch of that grass hung up over his door as a notice to the imps that he is not "at home."

An Encounter with a Hobgoblin

I got myself into trouble in the year Pyong-sin, and was locked up; a military man by the name of Choi Won-so, who was captain of the guard, was involved in it and locked up as well. We often met in prison and whiled away the hours talking together. On a certain day the talk turned to goblins, when Captain Choi said, "When I was young I met with a hobgoblin, which, by the fraction of a hair, almost cost me my life. A strange case indeed!"

I asked him to tell me of it, when he replied, "I had originally no home in Seoul, but hearing of a vacant place in Belt Town, I made application and got it. We went there, my father and the rest of the family occupying the inner quarters, while I lived in the front room.

"One night, late, when I was half asleep, the door suddenly opened, and a woman came in and stood just before the lamp. I saw her clearly, and knew that she was from the home of a scholar friend, for I had seen her before and had been greatly attracted by her beauty, but had never had a chance to meet her. Now, seeing her enter the room thus, I greeted her gladly, but she made no reply.

I arose to take her by the hand, when she began walking backwards, so that my hand never reached her. I rushed towards her, but she hastened her backward pace, so that she eluded me. We reached the gate, which she opened with a rear kick, and I followed on after, till she suddenly disappeared. I searched on all sides, but not a trace was there of her. I thought she had merely hidden herself, and never dreamed of anything else.

"On the next night she came again and stood before the lamp just as she had done the night previous. I got up and again tried to take hold of her, but again she began her peculiar pace backwards, till she passed out at the gate and disappeared just as she had done the day before. I was once more surprised and disappointed, but did not think of her being a hobgoblin.

"A few days later, at night, I had lain down, when suddenly there was a sound of crackling paper overhead from above the ceiling. A forbidding, creepy sound it seemed in the midnight. A moment later a curtain was let down that divided the room into two parts. Again, later, a large fire of coals descended right in front of me, while an immense heat filled the place. Where I was seemed all on fire, with no way of escape possible. In terror for my life, I knew not what to do. On the first cockcrow of morning the noise ceased, the curtain went up, and the fire of coals was gone. The place was as though swept with a broom, so clean from every trace of what had happened.

"The following night I was again alone, but had not yet undressed or lain down, when a great stout man suddenly opened the door and came in. He had on his head a soldier's felt hat, and on his body a blue tunic like one of the underlings of the yamen. He took hold of me and tried to drag me out. I was then young and vigorous, and had no intention of yielding to him, so we entered into a tussle. The moon was bright and the night clear, but I, unable to hold my own, was pulled out into the court. He lifted me up and swung me round and round, then went up to the highest terrace and threw me down, so that I was terribly stunned. He stood in front of me and kept me a prisoner. There was a garden to the rear of the house, and a wall round it. I looked, and within the wall were a dozen or so people. They were all dressed in military hats and coats, and they kept shouting out, 'Don't hurt him, don't hurt him.'

"The man that mishandled me, however, said in reply, 'It's none of your business, none of your business'; but they still kept up the cry, 'Don't hurt him, don't hurt him'; and he, on the other hand, cried, 'Never you mind; none of your business.' They shouted, 'The man is a gentleman of the military class; do not hurt him.'

"The fellow merely said in reply, 'Even though he is, it's none of your business'; so he took me by the two hands and flung me up into the air, till I went half way and more to heaven. Then in my fall I went shooting past Kyong-ki Province, past Choong-cheong, and at last fell to the ground in Cheolla. In my flight through space I saw all the county towns of the three provinces as clear as day. Again in Cheolla he tossed me up once more. Again I went shooting up into the sky and falling northward, till I found myself at home, lying stupefied below the verandah terrace. Once more I could hear the voices of the group in the garden shouting, 'Don't hurt him—hurt him.' But the man said, 'None of your business—your business.'

"He took me up once more and flung me up again, and away I went speeding off to Cheolla, and back I came again, two or three times in all.

"Then one of the group in the garden came forward, took my tormentor by the hand and led him away. They all met for a little to talk and laugh over the matter, and then scattered and were gone, so that they were not seen again.

"I lay motionless at the foot of the terrace till the following morning, when my father found me and had me taken in hand and cared for, so that I came to, and we all left the haunted house, never to go back."

Note: There are various reasons by which a place may be denominated a "haunted house." The fact that there are hobgoblins in it makes it haunted. If a good or "superior man" enters such a place the goblins move away, and no word of being haunted will be heard. Choi saw the goblin and was greatly injured.

I understand that it is not only a question of men fearing the goblins, but they also fear men. The fact that there are so few people that they fear is the saddest case of all. Choi was afraid of the goblins, that is why they troubled him.

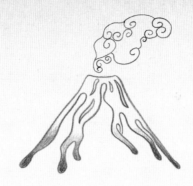

The Great Stone
Fire Eater

Ages ago, there lived a great Fire Spirit inside of a mountain to the southwest of Seoul, the capital of Korea. He was always hungry and his food was anything that would burn. He devoured trees, forests, dry grass, wood, and whatever he could get hold of. When those were not within his reach, he ate stones and rocks. He enjoyed the flames, but threw the hard stuff out of his mouth in the form of lava.

This Fire Monster spent most of his time in a huge volcano some distance away, but in sight of the capital. The city people used to watch the smoke coming out of the crater by day and issuing in red fire, between sunset and sunrise, until all the heavens seemed in flames. Then, they said, the Fire Spirit was lighting up his palace. On cloudy nights the inside of the volcano glowed like a furnace. The molten mass inside the crater was reflected on the clouds, so that one could almost see into the monster's belly.

But nothing tasted so good to the Fire Eater as things which men built, such as houses, stables, fences, and general property. A special tidbit, that he longed to swallow, was the royal palace.

Looking out of its crater one day, he saw the king's palace all silver bright and brand new, rising in the city of Seoul. Thereupon he chuckled, and said to himself, for he was very happy:

"There's a feast for me! I'll just walk out of my mountain home and eat up that dainty morsel. I wonder how the king will like it."

But the Fire Spirit was in no hurry. He felt sure of his meal. So he waited until his friend, the South Wind, was prepared to join him.

"Let me know when you're ready," said the Fire Spirit to the South Wind, "and we'll have a splendid blaze. We'll go up at night and enjoy a lively dance before they can get a drop of water on us. Don't let the rain clouds know anything about our picnic."

The South Wind promised easily, for she was always glad to have a frolic.

So when the sun went down and it was dark, the Fire Spirit climbed out of his rocky home in the volcano and strode toward Seoul. The South Wind pranced and capered with him until the streets of the capital were so gusty that no one with a wide-brimmed hat dared go outdoors, lest, in a lively puff, he might lose his headgear. As for the men in mourning, who wear straw hats a yardstick wide and as big and deep as washtubs, they locked themselves up at home and played checkers. By the time all the palace guards were asleep the Fire Spirit was ready. He said to the South Wind:

"Blow, blow, your biggest blast, as I begin to touch the roofs of the smaller houses. This will whet my appetite for the palace, and then together we'll eat them all up."

Not till they heard a mighty roar and crackling did the people in Seoul push back their paper windows to find out what was the matter. Oh, what a blaze! It seemed to mount to heaven with red tongues that licked the stars. Those who could see in the direction of the palace supposed the sun had risen, but soon the crash of falling roofs and mighty columns of smoke and flame, with clouds of sparks, told the terrible story. By the time the sun did rise, there was nothing but a level waste of ashes, where the large buildings had been. Even the smoke had been driven away by the wind.

When the king and his people in the palace enclosure, who had saved their lives by running fast, thought over their loss, they began to plan how to stop the Fire Monster, when he should take it into his head to saunter forth on

another walk and gobble up the king's
dwelling.

A council of wise men was called to decide
upon the question. Many long heads were bowed
in hard thought over the matter. All the firemen,
stonecutters, fortune tellers, dragon tamers, geomancers
and people skilled in preventing conflagrations were invited to give their advice
about the best way to fight the hungry Fire Demon.

After weeks spent in pondering the problem they all agreed that a dragon
from China should be brought over to Korea. If kept in a swamp and fed well,
he would surely prevent the Fire Imp from rambling too near Seoul. Besides,
the dragon knew how to amuse and persuade the South Wind not to join in the
mischief.

So, at tremendous cost and trouble, one of China's biggest dragons, capable of
making rain and of spouting tons of water on its enemies, was shipped over and
kept in a swamp. It was honored with a royal decoration, allowed to wear a string
of amber beads over its ear, given a horsehair hat, a nobleman's girdle and fed
all the turnips it desired to eat. In every way it was treated as the king's favorite.

But it was all in vain. Money and favor were alike wasted. The petted dragon
made it rain too often, so that the land was soaked. Then when told not to do
this, it grew sulky and neglected its duty. Finally it became fat and lazy and one
night fell asleep when it ought to have been on guard, for the winds were out
on a dance.

Seeing his
jailer thus caught
napping, the Fire Imp
leaped out of its volcano prison,
rode quickly on the South Wind to Seoul and in a
few hours had again swallowed the royal palace. There was nothing seen next day except ashes, which the Fire Monster cared no more for than we for nutshells when the kernels are eaten up.

With big tears in their eyes, the king and his wise men met together again to decide on a new scheme to keep off the Fire Imp. They were ready to drown him, or to see him get eaten up, because he had twice swallowed up the palace. They sent the Chinese dragon home and this time, besides the fortune tellers and the stonecutters, the well-diggers were invited also. For many days the wise men studied maps, talked of geography, looked at mountains, valleys, and the volcano, and studied air currents. Finally one man, famous for his deep learning about wood and water, forests and rivers, spoke thus:

"It is evident that the fire has always come from the southwest and up this valley," pointing to a map.

"True, true," shouted all the wise men.

"Well, right in his path let us dig a big pond, a regular artificial lake and very deep, into which the Fire Monster will tumble. This will put him out and he can get no further."

"Agreed, agreed," shouted the wise men in chorus. "Why did we not think of this before?"

All the skillful diggers of wells and ditches were summoned to the capital. With shovel and spade they worked for weeks. Then they let in water from the river until the pond was full.

So everybody in Seoul went to bed thinking that the king's palace was now surely safe.

But the Fire Imp, seeing the dragon gone and his opportunity come, climbed out of his volcano and moved out for another meal. This time, the South Wind was busy elsewhere and could not go with him. So he went alone, but coming to the pond, tumbled and wet himself so badly that he was chilled and nearly put out when he got to the palace, which was only half burned. So he went home growling and hungry.

Again the wise men were called and the first thing they did was to thank the boss well-digger, who had made the pond. The king summoned him into his presence to confer rank upon him and his children. He was presented with four rolls of silk, forty pounds of white ginseng, a tiger-skin robe, sixty dried chestnuts and forty-four strings of copper cash. Loaded with such wealth and honors, the man fell on his hands and knees and thanked His Majesty profusely.

Then they called the master stonecutter or chief of the guild and asked him if he could chisel out the figure of a beast that could eat flames and be ugly enough to scare away the Fire Imp.

The master had long hoped that he would be invited to rear this bit of sculpture, but hitherto the king and Court had feared it might cost too much.

So the order was given, and out of the heart of the mountains, a mighty block of white granite was loosed and brought to Seoul on rollers, pushed, pulled, and hoisted by thousands of laborers. Then, hidden behind canvas, to keep the matter secret, lest the Fire Imp should find it out, the workmen toiled. Hammers and chisels clinked, until on a certain day the Great Stone Flame Eater was ready to take his permanent seat in front of the palace gate, as guardian of the royal buildings and treasures.

The Fire Imp laughed when the South Wind told him of what the Koreans in the capital were doing, even though she warned him of the danger of his being eaten up.

"I shall walk out and see for myself anyhow," said the Fire Imp.

One night he crept out quietly and moved toward the city. He was nearly drowned in the pond, but plucking up courage, he went on until he was near the king's dwelling. Hearing the Fire Imp coming, the Great Flame Eater turned his head and licked his chops in anticipation of swallowing the Fire Imp whole, as a toad does a fly.

But one sight of the hideous stony monster was enough for the Fire Imp. There, before him, on a high pedestal was something never before seen in heaven or on earth. It had enormous fireproof scales like a salamander, with curly hair like asbestos and its mouth full of big fangs. It was altogether hideous enough to give even a Volcano Spirit a chill.

"Just think of those jaws snapping on me," said the Fire Imp to himself, as he looked at them and the fangs. "I do believe that creature is half alligator and half water-tortoise. I had better go home. No dinner this time!"

So by his freezing glance alone, the Great Flame Eater frightened away the Fire Imp, so that he never came again and the royal palace was not once burned. Today the ugly brute still keeps watch. You have only to look at him to enjoy this story.

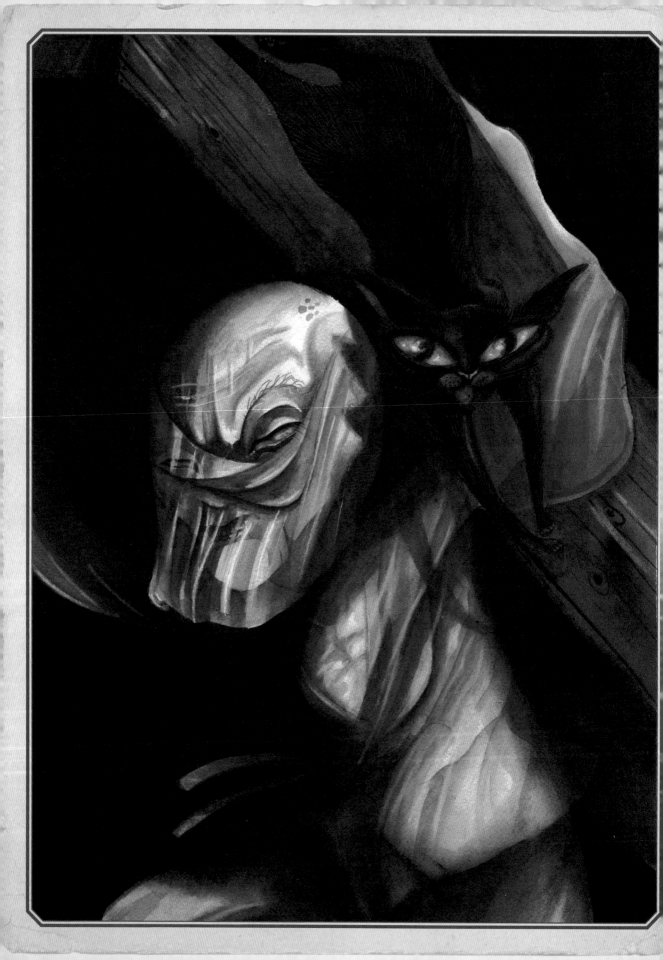

Cats and the Dead

About two and a half centuries ago a boy, who later became the great scholar Sa Cha, went to bed one night after a hard day's work on his Chinese. He had not been asleep long when he awoke with a start. The moon was shining in at the window and dimly lighting the room. Something was moving just outside the door. He lay still and listened. The door swung open of its own accord and a tall black object came gliding into the room and took its place in the corner silently. The boy mastered his fear and continued gazing into the darkness at his ominous visitor. He was a very strong-minded lad and after a while, seeing that the black ghost made no movement, he turned over and went to sleep. The moment he awoke in the morning he turned his eyes to the corner and there stood his visitor still. It was a great black coffin standing on end with the lid nailed on and evidently containing its intended occupant.

The boy gazed at it a long while and at last a look of relief came over his face. He called in his servant and said:

"Go down to the village and find out who has lost a corpse."

Soon the servant came running back with the news that the whole village was in an uproar. A funeral had been in progress but the watchers by the coffin had fallen asleep and when they awoke coffin and corpse had disappeared.

"Go and tell the chief mourner to come here."

When that excited individual appeared, the boy called him into the room and, pointing to the corner, said quietly, "What is that?"

The hemp-clad mourner gazed in wonder and consternation. "That? That's my father's coffin. What have you been doing? You've stolen my father's body and disgraced me forever."

The boy smiled and said, "How could I bring it here? It came of its own accord. I awoke in the night and saw it enter." The mourner was incredulous and angry.

"Now I will tell you why it came here," said the boy. "You have a cat in your house and it must be that it jumped over the coffin. This was such an offense to the dead that by some occult power, coffin, corpse and all came here to be safe from further insult. If you don't believe it send for your cat and we will see." The challenge was too direct to refuse and a servant was sent for the cat. Meanwhile the mourner tried to lay the coffin down on its side, but, with all his strength, he could not budge it an inch. The boy came up to it and gave it three strokes with his hand on the left side and a gentle push. The dead recognized the master hand and the coffin was easily laid on its side. When the cat arrived and was placed in the room the coffin of its own accord rose on end again, a position in which it was impossible for the cat to jump over it. The wondering mourner accepted the explanation and that day the corpse was laid safely in the ground. But to this day the watchers beside the dead are particularly careful to see that no cat enters the mortuary chamber lest it disturb the peace of the deceased.

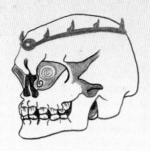

The King of Hell

In Yon-nan County, Hwanghae Province, there was a certain literary graduate whose name I have forgotten. He fell ill one day and remained in his room, leaning helplessly against his armrest. Suddenly several spirit soldiers appeared to him, saying, "The Governor of the lower hell has ordered your arrest," so they bound him with a chain about his neck, and led him away. They journeyed for many hundreds of miles, and at last reached a place that had a very high wall. The spirits then took him within the walls and went on for a long distance.

There was within this enclosure a great structure whose height reached to heaven. They arrived at the gate, and the spirits who had him in hand led him in, and when they entered the inner courtyard they laid him down on his face.

Glancing up he saw what looked like a king seated on a throne; grouped about him on each side were attendant officers. There were also scores of secretaries and soldiers going and coming on pressing errands. The King's appearance was most terrible, and his commands such as to fill one with awe. The graduate felt the perspiration break out on his back, and he dared not look up. In a little a secretary came forward, stood in front of the raised dais to transmit commands, and the King asked, "Where do you come from? What is your name? How old are you? What do you do for a living? Tell me the truth now, and no dissembling."

The scholar, frightened to death, replied, "My clan name is So-and-So, and my given name is So-and-So. I am so old, and I have lived for several generations at Yon-nan, Hwanghae Province. I am stupid and ill-equipped by nature, so have not done anything special. I have heard all my life that if you say your beads with love and pity in your heart you will escape hell, and so have given my time to calling on the Buddha, and dispensing alms."

The secretary, hearing this, went at once and reported it to the King. After some time he came back with a message, saying, "Come up closer to the steps, for you are not the person intended. It happens that you bear the same name and you have thus been wrongly arrested. You may go now."

The scholar joined his hands and made a deep bow. Again the secretary transmitted a message from the King, saying, "My house, when on earth, was in such a place in such and such a ward of Seoul. When you go back I want to send a message by you. My coming here is long, and the outer coat I wear is worn to shreds. Ask my people to send me a new outer coat. If you do so I shall be greatly obliged, so see that you do not forget."

The scholar said, "Your Majesty's message given me thus direct I shall pass on without fail, but the ways of the two worlds, the dark world and the light, are so different that when I give the message the hearers will say I am talking nonsense. True, I'll give it just as you have commanded, but what about if they refuse to listen? I ought to have some evidence as proof to help me out."

The King made answer, "Your words are true, very true. This will help you: When I was on earth," said he, "one of my head buttons that I wore had a broken edge, and I hid it in the third volume of the Book of History. I alone know of it, no one else in the world. If you give this as a proof they will listen."

The head button is the insignia of rank, and is consequently a valuable heirloom in a Korean home. The scholar replied, "That will be satisfactory, but again, how shall I do in case they make the new coat?"

The reply was, "Prepare a sacrifice, offer the coat by fire, and it will reach me."

He then bade goodbye, and the King sent with him two soldier guards. He asked the soldiers, as they came out, who the one seated on the throne was. "He is the King of Hades," said they; "his surname is Pak and his given name is Oo."

They arrived at the bank of a river, and the two soldiers pushed him into the water. He awoke with a start, and found that he had been dead for three days.

When he recovered from his sickness he came up to Seoul, searched out the house indicated, and made careful inquiry as to the name, finding that it was no other than Pak Oo. Pak Oo had two sons, who at that time had graduated and were holding office. The graduate wanted to see the sons of this King of Hades, but the gatekeeper would not let him in. Therefore he stood before the red gate waiting helplessly till the sun went down. Then came out from the inner quarters of the house an old servant, to whom he earnestly made petition that he might see the master. On being thus requested, the servant returned and reported it to the master, who, a little later, ordered him in. On entering, he saw two gentlemen who seemed to be chiefs. They had him sit down, and then questioned him as to who he was and what he had to say.

He replied, "I am a student living in Yon-nan County, Hwanghae Province. On such and such a day I died and went into the other world, where your honorable father gave me such and such a commission."

The two listened for a little and then, without waiting to hear all that he had to say, grew very angry and began to scold him, saying, "How dare such a scarecrow as you come into our house and say such things as these? This is stuff and nonsense that you talk. Pitch him out," they shouted to the servants.

He, however, called back saying, "I have a proof; listen. If it fails, why then, pitch me out."

One of the two said, "What possible proof can you have?" Then the scholar told with great exactness and care the story of the head button.

The two, in astonishment over this, had the book taken down and examined, and sure enough in Vol. III of the Book of History was the button referred to. Not a single particular had failed. It proved to be a button that they had missed after the death of their father, and that they had searched for in vain.

Accepting the message now as true, they all entered upon a period of mourning.

The women of the family also called in the scholar and asked him specially of what he had seen. So they made the outer coat, chose a day, and offered it by fire before the ancestral altar. Three days after the sacrifice the scholar dreamed, and the family of Pak dreamed too, that the King of Hades had come and given to each one of them his thanks for the coat. They long kept the scholar at their home, treating him with great respect, and became his firm friends forever after.

Pak Oo was a great-grandson of Minister Pak Chom. While he held office he was honest and just and was highly honored by the people. When he was Mayor of Hae-ju there arose a dispute between him and the Governor, which proved also that Pak was the honest man.

When I was at Hae-ju, Choi Yu-chom, a graduate, told me this story.

The Essence of Life

It may not be generally known to zoologists and natural historians that if a fox lives five hundred years its life essence, or *chung-geui*, condenses or crystalizes into a jewel and lies in the mouth of the animal. Neither would Yu Sung-yong have known it had it not been for a fortunate conjunction of circumstances. He was a young man of twenty and unmarried, and he lived in the southern town of An-dong.

One day as he sat at study he looked up and saw a most beautiful woman pass by. He was simply fascinated and could not but follow her. This was very bad form indeed but he was hardly accountable for his actions.

The next day his old teacher looked at him sharply and upbraided him, and the young man confessed his fault but pled as his excuse that he had been virtually hypnotized. He told the old man that every time the woman opened her mouth to speak, something like a diamond flashed between her teeth. The old man gave a violent start and exclaimed:

"The next time you see her, get possession of that jewel and swallow it instantly in spite of her tears."

A few days after, the fair vision passed his window again and as before he felt the mesmeric attraction, but he followed this time with a fixed purpose. He overtook the woman and entered into conversation with her as before, during the course of which he said:

"What is that beautiful jewel that I see in your mouth?"

"Ah, I mustn't tell you that," she answered. He pretended to be much offended.

"Let me see it just once," he said. She took it from her mouth and held it up between her thumb and finger. The ungallant Yu snatched it from her and swallowed it in a trice. The woman uttered a piercing scream and fell to the ground writhing as if in agony and weeping in a most heartrending way. Yu was almost sorry for what he had done but when he saw the form of the woman begin to assume the shape of a white fox his pity was changed to exultation. The fox slunk away up the hill and Yu went home. He had swallowed the essence of life and from that day on he had but to read a book once to master it. One glance at a page and he could repeat every word by heart. After passing before a line of ten thousand men he could tell, the next time he passed, whether the position of any one of them had been changed. It hardly need be said that he became the most famous scholar in the land.

But he had no wife, and it was high time that his bachelor days should be finished. One day as he was on his way to Seoul he stopped at an inn by the Han River. The innkeeper was a gentleman in reduced circumstances, and that night his young and clever daughter dreamed that she saw a dragon climbing a willow. In the morning she saw through a hole in the window the young man Yu standing in the yard. She was much taken with his appearance and so far set aside the dictates of modesty as to ask her father what his name was.

"His name is Yu Sung-yong, I believe."

"Is it possible?" she cried. "Why, that means willow becomes dragon." Then she told her dream. The father saw the point and approached the young man with a proposition that needed no urging, after he had once accidentally caught a glimpse of the girl's face. And the wedding came off all in good time.

The Enchanted Wine Jug

In ancient times there lived an old gray-haired man by the river's bank where the ferryboats land. He was poor but honest, and being childless, and compelled to earn his own food, he kept a little wine shop, which, small though it was, possessed quite a local reputation, for the aged proprietor would permit no quarrelling on his premises, and sold only one brand of wine, and this was of really excellent quality. He did not keep a pot of broth simmering over the coals at his door to tempt the passerby, and thus increase his thirst on leaving. The old man rather preferred the customers who brought their little long-necked bottles, and carried the drink to their homes. There were some peculiarities—almost mysteries—about this little wine shop; the old man had apparently always been there, and had never seemed any younger. His wine never gave out, no matter how great might be the local thirst, yet he was never seen to make or take in a new supply; nor had he a great array of vessels in his shop. On the contrary, he always seemed to pour the wine out of the one and same old bottle, the long, slender neck of which was black and shiny from being so often tipped in his old hand while the generous, warming stream gurgled outward to the bowl. This had long ceased to be a matter of inquiry, however, and only upon the advent of a stranger of an inquiring mind would the subject be re-discussed. The neighbors were assured that the old man was thoroughly good, and that his wine was better. Furthermore, he sold it as reasonably as other men sold a much inferior article. And more than this, they did not care to know; or at least if they did once care, they had gotten over it, and were now content to let well enough alone.

I said the old man had no children. That is true, yet he had that which in a slight degree took the place of children, in that they were his daily care, his constant companions, and the partners of his bed and board. These deputy children were none other than a good-natured old dog, with laughing face and eyes, long silken ears that were ever on the alert, yet too soft to stand erect, a chunky neck, and a large round body covered with long soft tan hair and ending in a bushy tail. He was the very impersonation of canine wisdom and good nature, and seldom became ruffled unless he saw his master worried by the ill behavior of one of his patrons, or when a festive flea persisted in attacking him on all sides at once. His fellow, a cat, would sometimes assist in the onslaught, when the dog was about to be defeated and completely ruffled by his tormentor.

This "Thomas" was also a character in his own way, and though past the days when his chief ambition had been to catch his tail, he had such a strong vein of humor running through him that age could not subdue his frivolous propensities. He had been known to drop a dead mouse upon the dog's nose from the counter, while the latter was endeavoring to get a quiet nap; and then he would blow his tail up like a balloon, hump his back, and look utterly shocked at such conduct, as the startled dog nearly jumped out of his skin, and growling horribly, tore around as though he were either in chase of a wild beast or being chased by one.

This happy couple lived in the greatest contentment with the old man. They slept in the little kang room with him at night, and enjoyed the warm stone floor, with its slick oilpaper covering, as much as did their master. When the old man would go out on a mild moonlit night to enjoy a pipe of tobacco and gaze at the stars, his companions would rush out and announce to the world that they were not asleep, but ready to encounter any and every thing that the darkness might bring forth, so long as it did not enter their master's private court, of which they were in possession.

These two were fair-weather companions up to this time. They had not been with the old man when a bowl of rice was a luxury. Their days did not antedate the period of the successful wine shop history. The old man, however, often recalled those former days with a shudder, and thought with great complacency of the time when he had befriended a divine being, in the form of a weary human traveler, to whom he gave the last drink his jug contained, and how, when the contents of the little jug had gurgled down the stranger's throat in a long unbroken draft, the stranger had given him a trifling little thing that looked like a bit of amber, saying: "Drop this into your jug, old man, and so long as it remains there, you will never want for a drink." He did so; and sure enough the jug was heavy with something, so that he raised it to his lips, and—could he believe it! a most delicious stream of wine poured down his parched throat.

He took the jug down and peered into its black depths; he shook its sides, causing the elf within to dance and laugh aloud; and shutting his eyes, again he took another long draft; then meaning well, he remembered the stranger, and was about to offer him a drink, when he discovered that he was all alone, and began to wonder at the strange circumstance, and to think what he was to do. "I can't sit here and drink all the time, or I will be drunk, and some thief will carry away my jug. I can't live on wine alone, yet I dare not leave this strange thing while I seek for work."

Like many another to whom fortune has just come, he knew not for a time what to do with his good luck. Finally he hit upon the scheme of keeping a wine shop, the success of which we have seen, and have perhaps refused the old man credit for the wisdom he displayed in continuing on in a small scale, rather than in exciting unpleasant curiosity and official oppression, by turning up his jug and attempting to produce wine at wholesale. The dog and cat knew the secret, and had ever a watchful eye upon the jug, which was never for a moment out of sight of one of the three pairs of eyes.

As the brightest day must end in gloom, however, so was this pleasant state soon to be marred by a most sad and far-reaching accident.

One day the news flashed around the neighborhood that the old man's supply of wine was exhausted; not a drop remained in his jug, and he had no more with which to refill it. Each man on hearing the news ran to see if it were indeed true, and the little straw-thatched hut and its small court encircled by a mud wall were soon filled with anxious seekers after the truth. The old man admitted the statement to be true, but had little to say; while the dog's ears hung neglectedly over his cheeks, his eyes dropped, and he looked as though he might be asleep, but for the persistent manner in which he refused to lie down, but dignifiedly bore his portion of the sorrow sitting upright, but with bowed head.

"Thomas" seemed to have been charged with agitation enough for the whole family. He walked nervously about the floor till he felt that justice to his tail demanded a higher plane, where shoes could not offend, and then betook himself to the counter, and later to the beam which supported the roof, and made a sort of cats' and rats' attic under the thatch.

All condoled with the old man, and not one but regretted that their supply of cheap, good wine was exhausted. The old man offered no explanation, though he had about concluded in his own mind that, as no one knew the secret, he must have in some way poured the bit of amber into a customer's jug. But who possessed the jug he could not surmise, nor could he think of any way of reclaiming it. He talked the matter over carefully and fully to himself at night, and the dog and cat listened attentively, winking knowingly at each other, and puzzling their brains much as to what was to be done and how they were to assist their kind old friend.

At last the old man fell asleep, and then sitting down face to face by his side, the dog and cat began a discussion. "I am sure," said the cat, "that I can detect that thing if I only come within smelling distance of it; but how do we know where to look for it?" That was a puzzler, but the dog proposed that they make

a search through every house in the neighborhood. "We can go on a mere *koo kyong* (look see), you know, and while you call on the cats indoors, and keep your smellers open, I will *ye gi* (chat) with the dogs outside, and if you smell anything you can tell me."

The plan seemed to be the only good one, and it was adopted that very night. They were not cast down because the first search was unsuccessful, and continued their work night after night. Sometimes their calls were not appreciated, and in a few cases they had to clear the field by battle before they could go on with the search. No house was neglected, however, and in due time they had done the whole neighborhood, but with no success. They then determined that it must have been carried to the other side of the river, to which place they decided to extend their search as soon as the water was frozen over, so that they could cross on the ice, for they knew they would not be allowed in the crowded ferryboats; and while the dog could swim, he knew that the water was too icy for that. As it soon grew very cold, the river froze so solidly that bull carts, ponies, and all passed over on the ice, and so it remained for near two months, allowing the searching party to return each morning to their poor old master, who seemed completely broken up by his loss, and did not venture away from his door, except to buy the few provisions which his little fund of savings would allow.

Time flew by without bringing success to the faithful comrades, and the old man began to think they too were deserting him, as his old customers had done. It was nearing the time for the spring thaw and freshet, when one night as the cat was chasing around over the roof timbers, in a house away to the outside of the settlement across the river, he detected an odor that caused him to stop so suddenly as to nearly precipitate himself upon a sleeping man on the floor below. He carefully traced up the odor, and found that it came from a soapstone tobacco box that sat upon the top of a high clothes press nearby. The box was dusty with neglect, and "Thomas" concluded that the possessor had accidentally turned the coveted gem (for it was from that the odor came) out into his wine bowl, and, not knowing its nature, had put it into this stone box rather than throw it away. The lid was so securely fastened that the box seemed to be one solid piece, and in despair of opening it, the cat went out to consult the superior wisdom of the dog, and see what could be done. "I can't get up there," said the dog, "nor can you bring me the box, or I might break it."

"I cannot move the thing, or I might push it off, and let it fall to the floor and break," said the cat.

So after explaining the things they could not do, the dog finally hit upon a plan they might perhaps successfully carry out. "I will tell you," said he. "You go and see the chief of the rat guild in this neighborhood, tell him that if he will help you in this matter, we will both let him alone for ten years, and not hurt even a mouse of them."

"But what good is that going to do?"

"Why, don't you see, that stone is no harder than some wood, and they can take turns at it till they gnaw a hole through, then we can easily get the gem."

The cat bowed before the marvelous judgment of the dog, and went off to accomplish the somewhat difficult task of obtaining an interview with the master rat. Meanwhile the dog wagged his ears and tail, and strode about with a swinging stride, in imitation of the great *yang ban*, or official, who occasionally walked past his master's door, and who seemed to denote by his haughty gait his superiority to other men. His importance made him impudent, and when the cat returned, to his dismay, he found his friend engaged in a genuine fight with a lot of curs who had dared to intrude upon his period of self-congratulation. "Thomas" mounted the nearest wall, and howled so lustily that the inmates of the house, awakened by the uproar, came out and dispersed the contestants.

The cat had found the rat, who, upon being assured of safety, came to the mouth of his hole, and listened attentively to the proposition. It is needless to say he accepted it, and a contract was made forthwith. It was arranged that work was to begin at once, and be continued by relays as long as they could work undisturbed, and when the box was perforated, the cat was to be summoned.

The ice had now broken up and the pair could not return home very easily, so they waited about the neighborhood for some months, picking up a scant living, and making many friends and not a few enemies, for they were a proud pair, and ready to fight on provocation.

It was warm weather, when, one night, the cat almost forgot his compact as he saw a big fat rat slinking along towards him. He crouched low and dug his long claws into the earth, while every nerve seemed on the jump; but before he was ready to spring upon his prey, he fortunately remembered his contract. It was just in time, too, for as the rat was none other than the other party to the contract, such a mistake at that time would have been fatal to their object.

The rat announced that the hole was completed, but was so small at the inside end that they were at a loss to know how to get the gem out, unless the cat could reach it with his paw. Having acquainted the dog with the good news, the cat hurried off to see for himself. He could introduce his paw, but as the object was at the other end of the box he could not quite reach it. They were in a dilemma, and were about to give up, when the cat went again to consult with the dog. The latter promptly told them to put a mouse into the box, and let him bring out the gem. They did so, but the hole was too small for the little fellow and his load to get out at the same time, so that much pushing and pulling had to be done before they were successful. They got it safely at last, however, and gave it at once to the dog for safekeeping. Then, with much purring and wagging of

tails, the contract of friendship was again renewed, and the strange party broke up; the rats to go and jubilate over their safety, the dog and cat to carry the good news to their mourning master.

Again canine wisdom was called into play in devising a means for crossing the river. The now happy dog was equal to such a trifling thing as this, however, and instructed the cat that he must take the gem in his mouth, hold it well between his teeth, and then mount his (the dog's) back, where he could hold on firmly to the long hair of his neck while he swam across the river. This was agreed upon, and arriving at the river they put the plan into execution. All went well until, as they neared the opposite bank, a party of schoolchildren chanced to notice them coming, and, after their amazement at the strange sight wore away, they burst into uproarious laughter, which increased the more they looked at the absurd sight. They clapped their hands and danced with glee, while some fell on the ground and rolled about in an exhaustion of merriment at seeing a cat astride a dog's back being ferried across the river.

The dog was too weary, and consequently matter-of-fact, to see much fun in it, but the cat shook his sides till his agitation caused the dog to take in great gulps of water in attempting to keep his head up. This but increased the cat's merriment, till he broke out in a laugh as hearty as that of the children, and in doing so dropped the precious gem into the water. The dog, seeing the sad accident, dove at once for the gem; regardless of the cat, who could not let go in time to escape, and was dragged down under the water. Sticking his claws into the dog's skin, in his agony of suffocation, he caused him so much pain that he missed the object of his search, and came to the surface.

The cat got ashore in some way, greatly angered at the dog's rude conduct. The latter, however, cared little for that, and as soon as he had shaken the water from his hide, he made a lunge at his unlucky companion, who had lost the results of a half year's faithful work in one moment of foolishness.

Dripping like a "drowned cat," "Thomas" was, however, able to climb a tree, and there he stayed till the sun had dried the water from his fur, and he had spat the water from his innards in the constant spitting he kept up at his now enemy, who kept barking ferociously about the tree below. The cat knew that the dog was dangerous when aroused, and was careful not to descend from his perch till the coast was clear; though at one time he really feared the ugly boys would knock him off with stones as they passed. Once down, he has ever since been careful to avoid the dog, with whom he has never patched up the quarrel. Nor does he wish to do so, for the very sight of a dog causes him to recall that horrible cold ducking and the day spent up a tree, and involuntarily he spits as though still filled with river-water, and his tail blows up as it had never learned to do till the day when for so long its damp and draggled condition would not permit of its assuming the haughty shape. This accounts for the scarcity of cats and the popularity of dogs in Korea.

The dog did not give up his efforts even now. He dove many times in vain, and spent most of the following days sitting on the river's bank, apparently lost in thought. Thus the winter found him—his two chief aims apparently being to find the gem and to kill the cat. The latter kept well out of his way, and the ice now covered the place where the former lay hidden. One day he spied a man spearing fish through a hole in the ice, as was very common. Having a natural desire to be around where anything eatable was being displayed, and feeling a sort of proprietorship in the particular part of the river where the man was fishing, and where he himself had had such a sad experience, he went down and looked on. As a fish came up, something natural seemed to greet his nostrils, and then, as the man lay down his catch, the dog grabbed it and rushed off in the greatest haste. He ran with all his might to his master, who, poor man, was now at the end of his string (coin in Korea is perforated and strung on a string), and was almost reduced to begging. He was therefore delighted when his faithful old friend brought him so acceptable a present as a fresh fish. He at once commenced dressing it, but when he slit it open, to his infinite joy, his long-lost gem fell out of the fish's belly. The dog was too happy to contain himself, but jumping upon his master, he licked him with his tongue, and struck him with his paws, barking meanwhile as though he had again treed the cat.

As soon as their joy had become somewhat natural, the old man carefully placed the gem in his trunk, from which he took the last money he had, together with some fine clothes—relics of his more fortunate days. He had feared he must soon pawn these clothes, and had even shown them to the brokers. But now he took them out to put them on, as his fortune had returned to him. Leaving the fish baking on the coals, he donned his fine clothes, and taking his last money, he went and purchased wine for his feast, and for a beginning; for he knew that once he placed the gem back in the jug, the supply of wine would not cease. On his return he and the good dog made a happy feast of the generous fish, and the old man completely recovered his spirits when he had quaffed deeply of the familiar liquid to which his mouth was now such a stranger. Going to his trunk directly, he found to his amazement that it contained another suit of clothes exactly like the first ones he had removed, while there lay also a broken string of cash of just the amount which he had previously taken out.

Sitting down to think, the whole truth dawned upon him, and he then saw how he had abused his privilege before in being content to use his talisman simply to run a wine shop, while he might have had money and everything else in abundance by simply giving the charm a chance to work.

Acting upon this principle, the old man eventually became immensely wealthy, for he could always duplicate anything with his piece of amber. He carefully tended his faithful dog, who never in his remaining days molested a rat, and never lost an opportunity to attack every cat he saw.

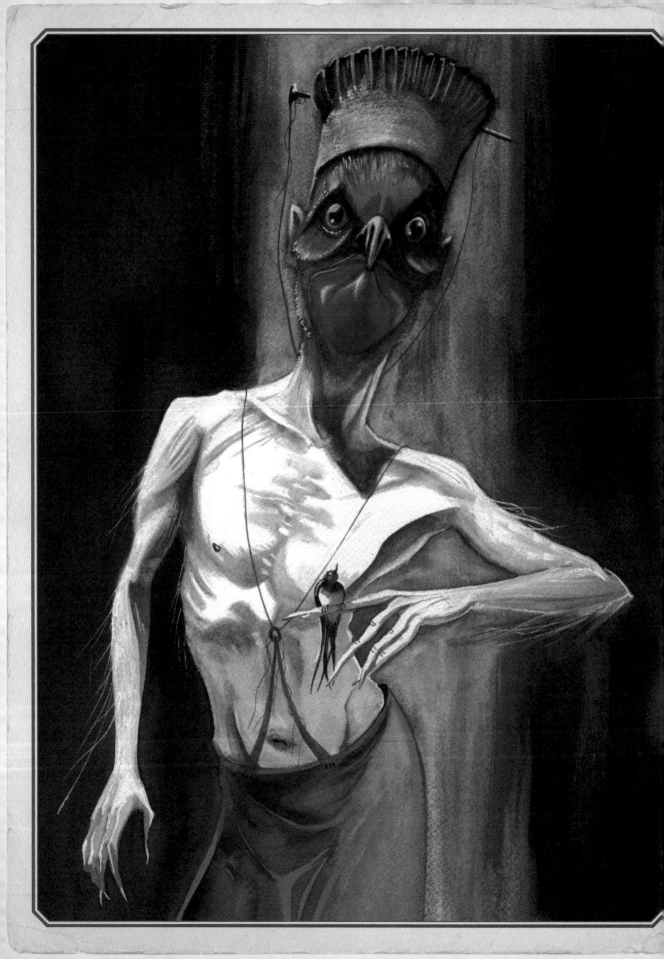

The Swallow King's Rewards

I.

In the province of Cheolla, in Southern Korea, lived two brothers. One was very rich, the other very poor. For in dividing the inheritance, the elder brother, instead of taking the father's place, and providing for his younger brother, kept the whole property to himself, allowing his younger brother nothing at all, and reducing him to a condition of abject misery. Both men were married. Nahl Bo, the elder, had many concubines, in addition to his wife, but had no children; while Hyung Bo had but one wife and several children. The former's wives were continually quarrelling; the latter lived in contentment and peace with his wife, each endeavoring to help the other bear the heavy burdens circumstances had placed upon them. The elder brother lived in a fine, large compound, with warm, comfortable houses; the younger had built himself a hut of broom straw, the thatch of which was so poor that when it rained they were deluged inside, upon the earthen floor. The room was so small, too, that when Hyung Bo stretched out his legs in his sleep his feet were apt to be thrust through the wall. They had no kang, and had to sleep upon the cold dirt floor, where insects were so abundant as to often succeed in driving the sleepers out of doors.

They had no money for the comforts of life, and were glad when a stroke of good fortune enabled them to obtain the necessities. Hyung Bo worked whenever he could get work, but rainy days and dull seasons were a heavy strain upon them. The wife did plain sewing, and together they made straw sandals for the peasants and vendors. At fair time the sandal business was good, but then came a time when no more food was left in the house, the string for making the sandals was all used up, and they had no money for a new supply. Then the children cried to their mother for food, till her heart ached for them, and the father wandered off in a last attempt to get something to keep the breath of life in his family.

Not a grain of rice was left. A poor rat which had cast in his lot with this kind family, became desperate when, night after night, he chased around the little house without being able to find the semblance of a meal. Becoming distraught, he vented his despair in such loud squealing that he wakened the neighbors, who declared that the mouse said his legs were worn off running about in a vain search for a grain of rice with which to appease his hunger. The famine became so serious in the little home, that at last the mother commanded her son to go to his uncle and tell him plainly how distressed they were, and ask him to loan them enough rice to subsist on till they could get work, when they would surely return the loan.

The boy did not want to go. His uncle would never recognize him on the street, and he was afraid to go inside his house lest he should whip him. But the mother commanded him to go, and he obeyed. Outside his uncle's house were many cows, well fed and valuable. In pens he saw great fat pigs in abundance, and fowls were everywhere in great numbers. Many dogs also were there, and they ran barking at him, tearing his clothes with their teeth and frightening him so much that he was tempted to run; but speaking kindly to them, they quieted down, and one dog came and licked his hand as if ashamed of the conduct of the others. A female servant ordered him away, but he told her he was her master's nephew, and wanted to see him; whereupon she smiled but let him pass into an inner court, where he found his uncle sitting on the little veranda under the broad, overhanging eaves.

The man gruffly demanded, "who are you?" "I am your brother's son," he said. "We are starving at our house, and have had no food for three days. My father is away now trying to find work, but we are very hungry, and only ask you to loan us a little rice till we can get some to return you."

The uncle's eyes drew down to a point, his brows contracted, and he seemed very angry, so that the nephew began looking for an easy way of escape in case he should come at him. At last he looked up and said: "My rice is locked up, and I have ordered the granaries not to be opened. The flour is sealed and cannot be broken into. If I give you some cold victuals, the dogs will bark at you and try to take it from you. If I give you the leavings of the winepress, the pigs will be jealous and squeal at you. If I give you bran, the cows and fowls will take after you. Get out, and let me never see you here again." So saying, he caught the poor boy by the collar and threw him into the outer court, hurting him, and causing him to cry bitterly with pain of body and distress of mind.

At home the poor mother sat jogging her babe in her weak arms, and appeasing the other children by saying that brother had gone to their uncle for food, and soon the pot would be boiling and they would all be satisfied. When, hearing a footfall, all scrambled eagerly to the door, only to see the empty-handed, red-eyed boy coming along, trying manfully to look cheerful.

"Did your uncle whip you?" asked the mother, more eager for the safety of her son, than to have her own crying want allayed.

"No," stammered the brave boy. "He had gone to the capital on business," said he, hoping to thus prevent further questioning, on so troublesome a subject.

"What shall I do?" queried the poor woman, amidst the crying and moaning of her children. There was nothing to do but starve, it seemed. However, she thought of her own straw shoes, which were scarcely used, and these she sent to the market, where they brought three cash (3/15 of a cent). This pittance was invested equally in rice, beans, and vegetables; eating which they were relieved for the present, and with full stomachs the little ones fell to playing happily once more, but the poor mother was full of anxiety for the morrow.

Their fortune had turned, however, with their new lease of life, for the father returned with a bale of fagots he had gathered on the mountains, and with the proceeds of these the shoes were redeemed and more food was purchased. Bright and early the next morning both parents went forth in search of work. The wife secured employment winnowing rice. The husband overtook a boy bearing a pack, but his back was so blistered, he could with difficulty carry his burden. Hyung Bo adjusted the saddle of the pack frame to his own back, and carried it for the boy, who, at their arrival at his destination in the evening, gave his helper some cash, in addition to his lodging and meals. During the night, however, a gentleman wished to send a letter by rapid dispatch to a distant place, and Hyung Bo was paid well for carrying it.

Returning from this profitable errand, he heard of a very rich man, who had been seized by the corrupt local magistrate, on a false accusation, and was to be beaten publicly, unless he consented to pay a heavy sum as hush money. Hearing of this, Hyung went to see the rich prisoner, and arranged with him that he would act as his substitute for three thousand cash (two dollars). The man was very glad to get off so easily, and Hyung took the beating. He limped to his house, where his poor wife greeted him with tears and lamentations, for he was a sore and sorry sight indeed. He was cheerful, however, for he explained to them that this had been a rich day's work; he had simply submitted to a little whipping, and was to get three thousand cash for it.

The money did not come, however, for the fraud was detected, and the original prisoner was also punished. Being of rather a close disposition, the man seemed to think it unnecessary to pay for what did him no good. Then the wife cried indeed over her husband's wrongs and their own more unfortunate condition. But the husband cheered her, saying: "If we do right we will surely succeed." He was right. Spring was coming on, and he soon got work at plowing and sowing seed. They gave their little house the usual spring cleaning, and decorated the door with appropriate legends, calling upon the fates to bless with prosperity the little home.

With the spring came the birds from the south country, and they seemed to have a preference for the home of this poor family—as indeed did the rats and insects. The birds built their nests under the eaves. They were swallows, and as they made their little mud air-castles, Hyung Bo said to his wife: "I am afraid to have these birds build their nests there. Our house is so weak it may fall down, and then what will the poor birds do?" But the little visitors seemed not alarmed, and remained with the kind people, apparently feeling safe under the friendly roof.

By and by the little nests were full of commotion and bluster; the eggs had opened, and circles of wide opened mouths could be seen in every nest. Hyung and his children were greatly interested in this new addition to their family circle, and often gave them bits of their own scanty allowance of food, so that the birds became quite tame and hopped in and out of the hut at will.

One day, when the little birds were taking their first lesson in flying, Hyung was lying on his back on the ground, and saw a huge roof-snake crawl along and devour several little birds before he could arise and help them. One bird struggled from the reptile and fell, but, catching both legs in the fine meshes of a reed-blind, they were broken, and the little fellow hung helplessly within the snake's reach. Hyung hastily snatched it down, and with the help of his wife he bound up the broken limbs, using dried fish-skin for splints. He laid the little patient in a warm place, and the bones speedily united, so that the bird soon began to hop around the room, and pick up bits of food laid out for him. Soon the splints were removed, however, and he flew away, happily, to join his fellows.

The autumn came; and one evening—it was the ninth day of the ninth moon—as the little family were sitting about the door, they noticed the bird with the crooked legs sitting on the clothesline and singing to them.

"I believe he is thanking us and saying goodbye," said Hyung, "for the birds are all going south now."

That seemed to be the truth, for they saw their little friend no longer, and they felt lonely without the occupants of the now deserted nests. The birds, however, were paying homage to the king of birds in the bird-land beyond the frosts. And as the king saw the little crooked-legged bird come along, he demanded an explanation of the strange sight. Thereupon the little fellow related his narrow escape from a snake that had already devoured many of his brothers and cousins, the accident in the blind, and his rescue and subsequent treatment by a very poor but very kind man.

His bird majesty was very much entertained and pleased. He thereupon gave the little cripple a seed engraved with fine characters in gold, denoting that the seed belonged to the gourd family. This seed the bird was to give to his benefactor in the spring.

The winter wore away, and the spring found the little family almost as destitute as when first we described them. One day they heard a familiar birdsong, and, running out, they saw their little crooked-legged friend with something in its mouth, that looked like a seed. Dropping its burden to the ground, the little bird sang to them of the king's gratitude, and of the present he had sent, and then flew away.

Hyung picked up the seed with curiosity, and on one side he saw the name of its kind, on the other, in fine gold characters, was a message saying: "Bury me in soft earth, and give me plenty of water." They did so, and in four days the little shoot appeared in the fine earth. They watched its remarkable growth with eager interest as the stem shot up, and climbed all over the house, covering it up as a bower, and threatening to break down the frail structure with the added weight. It blossomed, and soon four small gourds began to form. They grew to an enormous size, and Hyung could scarcely keep from cutting them. His wife prevailed on him to wait till the frost had made them ripe, however, as then they could cut them, eat the inside, and make water-vessels of the shells, which they could then sell, and thus make a double profit. He waited, though with a poor grace, till the ninth moon, when the gourds were left alone, high upon the roof, with only a trace of the shriveled stems which had planted them there.

Hyung got a saw and sawed open the first huge gourd. He worked so long, that when his task was finished he feared he must be in a swoon, for out of the opened gourd stepped two beautiful boys, with fine bottles of wine and a table of jade set with dainty cups. Hyung staggered back and sought assurance of his wife, who was fully as dazed as was her husband. The surprise was somewhat relieved by one of the handsome youths stepping forth, placing the table before them, and announcing that the bird king had sent them with these presents to the benefactor of one of his subjects—the bird with broken legs. Ere they could answer, the other youth placed a silver bottle on the table, saying: "This wine will restore life to the dead." Another, which he placed on the table, would, he said, restore sight to the blind. Then going to the gourd, he brought two gold bottles. One contained a tobacco, which, being smoked, would give speech to the dumb, while the other gold bottle contained wine, which would prevent the approach of age and ward off death.

Having made these announcements, the pair disappeared, leaving Hyung and his wife almost dumb with amazement. They looked at the gourd, then at the little table and its contents, and each looked at the other to be sure it was not a dream. At length Hyung broke the silence, remarking that, as he was very hungry, he would venture to open another gourd, in the hope that it would be found full of something good to eat, since it was not so important for him to have something with which to restore life just now as it was to have something to sustain life with.

The next gourd was opened as was the first, when by some means out flowed all manner of household furniture, and clothing, with rolls upon rolls of fine silk and satin cloth, linen goods, and the finest cotton. The satin alone was far greater in bulk than the gourd had been, yet, in addition, the premises were literally strewn with costly furniture and the finest fabrics. They barely examined the goods now, their amazement having become so great that they could scarcely wait until all had been opened, and the whole seemed so unreal, that they feared delay might be dangerous. Both sawed away on the next gourd, when out came a body of carpenters, all equipped with tools and lumber, and, to their utter and complete amazement, began putting up a house as quickly and quietly as thought, so that before they could arise from the ground they saw a fine house standing before them, with courts and servants' quarters, stables, and granaries. Simultaneously a great train of bulls and ponies appeared, loaded down with rice and other products as tributes from the district in which the place was located. Others came bringing money tribute, servants, male and female, and clothing.

They felt sure they were in dreamland now, and that they might enjoy the exercise of power while it lasted, they began commanding the servants to put the goods away, the money in the *sahrang*, or reception room, the clothing in the *tarack*, or garret over the fireplace, the rice in the granaries, and animals in their stables. Others were sent to prepare a bath, that they might don the fine clothing before it should be too late. The servants obeyed, increasing the astonishment of the pair, and causing them to literally forget the fourth gourd in their amazed contemplation of the wondrous miracles being performed, and the dreamy air of satisfaction and contentment with which it surrounded them.

Their attention was called to the gourd by the servants, who were then commanded to carefully saw it open. They did so, and out stepped a maiden, as beautiful as were the gifts that had preceded her. Never before had Hyung looked on anyone who could at all compare with the matchless beauty and grace of the lovely creature who now stood so modestly and confidingly before him. He could find no words to express his boundless admiration, and could only stand in mute wonder and feast himself upon her beauty. Not so with his wife, however. She saw only a rival in the beautiful girl, and straightaway demanded who she was, whence she came, and what she wanted. The maid replied: "I am sent by the bird king to be this man's concubine." Whereupon the wife grew dark in the face, and ordered her to go whence she came and not see her husband again. She upbraided him for not being content with a house and estate, numbers of retainers and quantities of money, and declared this last trouble was all due to his greed in opening the fourth gourd.

Her husband had by this time found his speech, however, and severely reprimanding her for conducting herself in such a manner upon the receipt of such heavenly gifts, while yesterday she had been little more than a beggar, he commanded her to go at once to the women's quarters, where she should reign supreme, and never make such a display of her ill temper again, under penalty of being consigned to a house by herself. The maiden he gladly welcomed, and conducted her to apartments set aside for her.

II.

When Nahl Bo heard of the wonderful change taking place at his brother's establishment, he went himself to look into the matter. He found the report not exaggerated, and began to upbraid his brother with dishonest methods, which accusation the brother stoutly denied, and further demanded where, and of whom, he could steal a house, such rich garments, fine furniture, and have it removed in a day to the site of his former hovel. Nahl Bo demanded an explanation, and Hyung Bo frankly told him how he had saved the bird from the snake and had bound up its broken limbs, so that it recovered; how the bird in return brought him a seed engraved with gold characters, instructing him how to plant and rear it; and how, having done so, the four gourds were born on the stalk, and from them, on ripening, had appeared these rich gifts. The ill-favored brother even then persisted in his charges, and in a gruff, ugly manner accused Hyung Bo of being worse than a thief in keeping all these fine goods, instead of dutifully sharing them with his elder brother. This insinuation of undutiful conduct really annoyed Hyung Bo, who, in his kindness of heart, forgave this unbrotherly senior his former ill conduct, and thinking only of his own present good fortune, he kindly bestowed considerable gifts upon the undeserving brother, and doubtless would have done more but that the covetous man spied the fair maiden, and at once insisted on having her. This was too much even for the patient Hyung Bo, who refused with a determination remarkable for him. A quarrel ensued, during which the elder brother took his departure in a rage, fully determined to use the secret of his brother's success for all it was worth in securing rich gifts for himself.

Going home he struck at all the birds he could see, and ordered his servants to do the same. After killing many, he succeeded in catching one, and, breaking its legs, he took fish skin and bound them up in splints, laying the little sufferer in a warm place, till it recovered and flew away, bandages and all. The result was as expected. The bird being questioned by the bird king concerning its crooked legs, related its story, dwelling, however, on the man's cruelty in killing so many birds and then breaking its own legs. The king understood thoroughly, and gave the little cripple a seed to present to the wicked man on its return in the spring.

Springtime came, and one day, as Nahl Bo was sitting cross-legged in the little room opening on the veranda off his court, he heard a familiar birdsong. Dropping his long pipe, he threw open the paper windows, and there, sure enough, sat a crooked-legged bird on the clothesline, bearing a seed in its mouth. Nahl Bo would let no one touch it, but as the bird dropped the seed and flew away, he jumped out so eagerly that he forgot to slip his shoes on, and got his clean white stockings all befouled. He secured the seed, however, and felt that his fortune was made. He planted it carefully, as directed, and gave it his personal attention.

The vines were most luxurious. They grew with great rapidity, till they had well-nigh covered the whole of his large house and outbuildings. Instead of one gourd, or even four, as in the brother's case, the new vines bore twelve gourds, which grew and grew till the great beams of his house fairly groaned under their weight, and he had to block them in place to keep them from rolling off the roofs. He had to hire men to guard them carefully, for now that the source of Hyung Bo's riches was understood, everyone was anxious for a gourd. They did not know the secret, however, which Nahl Bo concealed through selfishness, and Hyung through fear that everyone would take to killing and maiming birds as his wicked brother had done.

Maintaining a guard was expensive, and the plant so loosened the roof tiles, by the tendrils searching for earth and moisture in the great layer of clay under the tiles, that the rainy season made great havoc with his house. Large portions of plaster from the inside fell upon the paper ceilings, which in turn gave way, letting the dirty water drip into the rooms, and making the house almost uninhabitable. At last, however, the plants could do no more harm; the frost had come, the vines had shriveled away, and the enormous ripe gourds were care-fully lowered, amid the yelling of a score of servants, as each seemed to get in the others' way trying to manipulate the ropes and poles with which the gourds were let down to the ground. Once inside the court, and the great doors locked, Nahl Bo felt relieved, and shutting out everyone but a carpenter and his assis-tant, he prepared for the great surprise which he knew must await him, in spite of his most vivid dreams.

The carpenter insisted upon the enormous sum of 1,000 cash for opening each gourd, and as he was too impatient to await the arrival of another, and as he expected to be of princely wealth in a few moments, Nahl Bo agreed to the exorbitant price. Whereupon, carefully bracing a gourd, the men began sawing it through. It seemed a long time before the gourd fell in halves. When it did, out came a party of rope dancers, such as perform at fairs and public places. Nahl Bo was unprepared for any such surprise as this, and fancied it must be some great mistake. They sang and danced about as well as the crowded condition of the court would allow, and the family looked on complacently, supposing that the band had been sent to celebrate their coming good fortune. But Nahl Bo soon had enough of this. He wanted to get at his riches, and seeing that the actors were about to stretch their ropes for a more extensive performance, he ordered them to cease and take their departure. To his amazement, however, they refused to do this, until he had paid them 5,000 cash for their trouble. "You sent for us and we came," said the leader. "Now pay us, or we will live with you till you do." There was no help for it, and with great reluctance and some fore-boding, he gave them the money and dismissed them. Then Nahl Bo turned to the carpenter, who chanced to be a man with an ugly visage, and a great cleft lip. "You," he said, "are the cause of all this. Before you entered this court these gourds were filled with gold, and your ugly face has changed it to beggars."

Number two was opened with no better results, for out came a body of Buddhist priests, begging for their temple, and promising many sons in return for offerings of suitable merit. Although disgusted beyond measure, Nahl Bo still had faith in the gourds, and to get rid of the priests, lest they should see his riches, he gave them also 5,000 cash.

As soon as the priests were gone, gourd number three was opened, with still poorer results, for out came a procession of paid mourners followed by a corpse borne by bearers. The mourners wept as loudly as possible, and all was in a perfect uproar. When ordered to go, the mourners declared they must have money for mourning, and to pay for burying the body. Seeing no possible help for it, 5,000 cash was finally given them, and they went out with the bier. Then Nahl Bo's wife came into the court, and began to abuse the cleft-lipped man for bringing upon them all this trouble. Whereupon the latter became angry and demanded his money that he might leave. They had no intention of giving up the search as yet, however, and, as it was too late to change carpenters, the ugly fellow was paid for the work already done, and given an advance on that yet remaining. He therefore set to work upon the fourth gourd, which Nahl Bo watched with feverish anxiety.

From this one there came a band of *gi sang*, or dancing girls. There was one woman from each province, and each had her song and dance. One sang of the *yang wang*, or wind god; another of the *wang jay*, or pan deity; one sang of the *sung ji*, or money that is placed as a christening on the roof tree of every house. There was the cuckoo song. The song of the ancient tree that has lived so long that its heart is dead and gone, leaving but a hollow space, yet the leaves spring forth every springtide. The song of laughter and mourning, with an injunction to see to it that the rice offering be made to the departed spirits. To the king of the sun and stars a song was sung. And last of all, one votary sang of the twelve months that make the year, the twelve hours that make the day, the thirty days that make the month, and of the new year's birth, as the old year dies, taking with it their ills to be buried in the past, and reminding all people to celebrate the New Year holidays by donning clean clothes and feasting on good food, that the following year may be to them one of plenty and prosperity. Having finished their songs and their graceful posturing and waving of their gay silk banners, the *gi sang* demanded their pay, which had to be given them, reducing the family wealth 5,000 cash more.

The wife now tried to persuade Nahl Bo to stop and not open more, but the cleft-lipped man offered to open the next for 500 cash, as he was secretly enjoying the sport. So the fifth was opened a little, when a yellow-looking substance was seen inside, which was taken to be gold, and they hurriedly opened it completely. But instead of gold, out came an acrobatic pair—being a strong man with a youth dressed to represent a girl. The man danced about, holding his young companion balanced upon his shoulders, singing meanwhile a song of an ancient king, whose riotous living was so distasteful to his subjects that he built him a cavernous palace, the floor of which was covered with quicksilver, the walls were decorated with jewels, and myriad lamps turned the darkness into day. Here were to be found the choicest viands and wines, with bands of music to entertain the feasters: most beautiful women; and he enjoyed himself most luxuriously until his enemy, learning the secret, threw open the cavern to the light of day, when all of the beautiful women immediately disappeared in the sun's rays.

Before he could get these people to discontinue their performance, Nahl Bo had to give them also 5,000 cash. Yet in spite of all his ill luck, he decided to open another. Which being done, a jester came forth, demanding the expense money for his long journey. This was finally given him, for Nahl Bo had hit upon what he deemed a clever expedient. He took the wise fool aside, and asked him to use his wisdom in pointing out to him which of these gourds contained gold. Whereupon the jester looked wise, tapped several gourds, and motioned to each one as being filled with gold.

The seventh was therefore opened, and a lot of yamen runners came forth, followed by an official. Nahl Bo tried to run from what he knew must mean an exorbitant "squeeze," but he was caught and beaten for his indiscretion. The official called for his valise, and took from it a paper, which his secretary read, announcing that Nahl Bo was the serf of this lord and must hereafter pay to him a heavy tribute. At this they groaned in their hearts, and the wife declared that even now the money was all gone, even to the last cash, while the rabble which had collected had stolen nearly everything worth removing. Yet the officer's servants demanded pay for their services, and they had to be given a note secured on the property before they would leave. Matters were now so serious that they could not be made much worse, and it was decided to open each remaining gourd, that if there were any gold they might have it.

When the next one was opened a bevy of *mudang* women (soothsayers) came forth, offering to drive away the spirit of disease and restore the sick to health. They arranged their banners for their usual dancing ceremony, brought forth their drums, with which to exorcise the demons, and called for rice to offer to the spirits and clothes to burn for the spirits' apparel.

"Get out!" roared Nahl Bo. "I am not sick except for the visitation of such as yourselves, who are forever burdening the poor, and demanding pay for your supposed services. Away with you, and befool some other *pah sak ye* (eight month's man—fool) if you can. I want none of your services."

They were no easier to drive away, however, than were the other annoying visitors that had come with his supposed good fortune. He had finally to pay them as he had the others; and dejectedly he sat, scarcely noticing the opening of the ninth gourd.

The latter proved to contain a juggler, and the exasperated Nahl Bo, seeing but one small man, determined to make short work of him. Seizing him by his topknot of hair, he was about to drag him to the door, when the dexterous fellow, catching his tormentor by the thighs, threw him headlong over his own back, nearly breaking his neck, and causing him to lie stunned for a time, while the expert bound him hand and foot, and stood him on his head, so that the wife was glad to pay the fellow and dismiss him ere the life should be departed from her lord.

On opening the tenth a party of blind men came out, picking their way with their long sticks, while their sightless orbs were raised towards the unseen heavens. They offered to tell the fortunes of the family. But, while their services might have been demanded earlier, the case was now too desperate for any such help. The old men tinkled their little bells, and chanted some poetry addressed to the four good spirits stationed at the four corners of the earth, where they patiently stand bearing the world upon their shoulders; and to the distant heavens that arch over and fold the earth in their embrace, where the two meet at the far horizon (as pictured in the Korean flag). The blind men threw their dice, and, fearing lest they should prophesy death, Nahl Bo quickly paid and dismissed them.

The next gourd was opened but a trifle, that they might first determine as to the wisdom of letting out its contents. Before they could determine, however, a voice like thunder was heard from within, and the huge form of a giant arose, splitting open the gourd as he came forth. In his anger he seized poor Nahl Bo and tossed him upon his shoulders as though he would carry him away. Whereupon the wife pled with tears for his release, and gladly gave an order for the amount of the ransom. After which the monster allowed the frightened man to fall to the ground, nearly breaking his aching bones in the fall.

The carpenter did not relish the sport any longer; it seemed to be getting entirely too dangerous. He thereupon demanded the balance of his pay, which they finally agreed to give him, providing he would open the last remaining gourd. For the desperate people hoped to find this at least in sufficient condition that they might cook or make soup of it, since they had no food left at all and no money, while the other gourds were so spoiled by the tramping of the feet of their unbidden guests, as to be totally unfit for food.

The man did as requested, but had only sawed a very little when the gourd split open as though it were rotten, while a most awful stench arose, driving everyone from the premises. This was followed by a gale of wind, so severe as to destroy the buildings, which, in falling, took fire from the kang, and while the once prosperous man looked on in helpless misery, the last of his remaining property was swept forever from him.

The seed that had brought prosperity to his honest, deserving brother had turned prosperity into ruin for the cruel, covetous Nahl Bo, who now had to subsist upon the charity of his kind brother, whom he had formerly treated so cruelly.

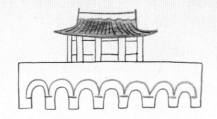

The Story of
Chang To-ryong

Taoism has been one of the great religions of Korea. Its main thought is expressed in the phrase *su-sim yon-song*, "to correct the mind and reform the nature"; while Buddhism's is *myong-sim kyon-song*, "to enlighten the heart and see the soul."

The desire of all Taoists is "eternal life," *chang-saeng pul-sa*; that of the Buddhists, to rid oneself of fleshly being. In the Taoist world of the genii, there are three great divisions: the upper genii, who live with God; the midway genii, who have to do with the world of angels and spirits; and the lower genii, who rule in sacred places on the earth, among the hills, just as we find in the story of Chang To-ryong.

In the days of King Chung-jong (1507–1526) there lived a beggar in Seoul, whose face was extremely ugly and always dirty. He was forty years of age or so, but still wore his hair down his back like an unmarried boy. He carried a bag over his shoulder, and went about the streets begging. During the day he went from one part of the city to the other, visiting each section, and when night came on he would huddle up beside someone's gate and go to sleep. He was frequently seen in Bell Street in company with the servants and underlings of the rich. They were great friends, he and they, joking and bantering as they met. He used to say that his name was Chang, and so they called him Chang To-ryong, *to-ryong* meaning an unmarried boy, son of the gentry. At that time the magician Chon U-chi, who was far-famed for his pride and arrogance, whenever he met Chang, in passing along the street, would dismount and prostrate himself most humbly. Not only did he bow, but he seemed to regard Chang with the greatest of fear, so that he dared not look him in the face. Chang, sometimes, without even inclining his head, would say, "Well, how goes it with you, eh?" Chon, with his hands in his sleeves, most respectfully would reply, "Very well, sir, thank you, very well." He had fear written on all his features when he faced Chang.

Sometimes, too, when Chon would bow, Chang would refuse to notice him at all, and go by without a word. Those who saw it were astonished, and asked Chon the reason. Chon said in reply, "There are only three spirit-men at present in Chosen, of whom the greatest is Chang To-ryong; the second is Cheung Puk-chang; and the third is Yun Se-pyong. People of the world do not know it, but I do. Such being the case, should I not bow before him and show him reverence?"

Those who heard this explanation, knowing that Chon himself was a strange being, paid no attention to it.

At that time in Seoul there was a certain literary undergraduate in office whose house joined hard on the street. This man used to see Chang frequently going about begging, and one day he called him and asked who he was, and why he begged. Chang made answer, "I was originally of a cultured family of Cheolla Province, but my parents died of typhus fever, and I had no brothers or relations left to share my lot. I alone remained of all my clan, and having no home of my own I have gone about begging, and have at last reached Seoul. As I am not skilled in any handicraft, and do not know Chinese letters, what else can I do?" The undergraduate, hearing that he was a scholar, felt very sorry for him, gave him food and drink, and refreshed him.

From this time on, whenever there was any special celebration at his home, he used to call Chang in and have him share it.

On a certain day when the master was on his way to office, he saw a dead body being carried on a stretcher off toward the Water Gate. Looking at it closely from the horse on which he rode, he recognized it as the corpse of Chang To-ryong. He felt so sad that he turned back to his house and cried over it, saying, "There are lots of miserable people on earth, but whoever saw one as miserable as poor Chang? As I reckon the time over on my fingers, he has been begging in Bell Street for fifteen years, and now he passes out of the city a dead body."

Twenty years and more afterwards the master had to make a journey through South Cheolla Province. As he was passing Ji ri Mountain, he lost his way and got into a maze among the hills. The day began to wane, and he could neither return nor go forward. He saw a narrow footpath, such as woodmen take, and turned into it to see if it led to any habitation. As he went along there were rocks and deep ravines. Little by little, as he advanced farther, the scene changed and seemed to become strangely transfigured. The farther he went the more wonderful it became. After he had gone some miles he discovered himself to be in another world entirely, no longer a world of earth and dust. He saw someone coming toward him dressed in ethereal green, mounted and carrying a shade, with servants accompanying. He seemed to sweep toward him with swiftness and without effort. He thought to himself, "Here is some high lord or other coming to meet me, but," he added, "how among these deeps and solitudes could a gentleman come riding so?" He led his horse aside and tried to withdraw into one of the groves by the side of the way, but before he could think to turn the man had reached him. The mysterious stranger lifted his two hands in salutation and inquired respectfully as to how he had been all this time. The master was speechless, and so astonished that he could make no reply. But the stranger smilingly said, "My house is quite near here; come with me and rest."

He turned, and leading the way seemed to glide and not to walk, while the master followed. At last they reached the place indicated. He suddenly saw before him great palace halls filling whole squares of space. Beautiful buildings they were, richly ornamented. Before the door attendants in official robes awaited them. They bowed to the master and led him into the hall. After passing a number of gorgeous, palace-like rooms, he arrived at a special one and ascended to the upper story, where he met a very wonderful person. He was dressed in shining garments, and the servants that waited on him were exceedingly fair. There were, too, children about, so exquisitely beautiful that it seemed none other than a celestial palace. The master, alarmed at finding himself in such a place, hurried forward and made a low obeisance, not daring to lift his eyes. But the host smiled upon him, raised his hands and asked, "Do you not know me? Look now." Lifting his eyes, he then saw that it was the same person who had come riding out to meet him, but he could not tell who he was. "I see you," said he, "but as to who you are I cannot tell."

The kingly host then said, "I am Chang To-ryong. Do you not know me?" Then as the master looked more closely at him he could see the same features. The outlines of the face were there, but all the imperfections had gone, and only beauty remained. So wonderful was it that he was quite overcome.

A great feast was prepared, and the honored guest was entertained. Such food, too, was placed before him as was never seen on earth. Angelic beings played on beautiful instruments and danced as no mortal eye ever looked upon. Their faces, too, were like pearls and precious stones.

Chang To-ryong said to his guest, "There are four famous mountains in Korea in which the genii reside. This hill is one. In days gone by, for a fault of mine, I was exiled to earth, and in the time of my exile you treated me with marked kindness, a favor that I have never forgotten. When you saw my dead body your pity went out to me; this, too, I remember. I was not dead then, it was simply that my days of exile were ended and I was returning home. I knew that you were passing this hill, and I desired to meet you and to thank you for all your kindness. Your treatment of me in another world is sufficient to bring about our meeting in this one." And so they met and feasted in joy and great delight.

When night came he was escorted to a special pavilion, where he was to sleep. The windows were made of jade and precious stones, and soft lights came streaming through them, so that there was no night. "My body was so rested and my soul so refreshed," said he, "that I felt no need of sleep."

When the day dawned a new feast was spread, and then farewells were spoken. Chang said, "This is not a place for you to stay long in; you must go. The ways differ of we genii and you men of the world. It will be difficult for us ever to meet again. Take good care of yourself and go in peace." He then called a servant to accompany him and show the way. The master made a low bow and withdrew. When he had gone but a short distance he suddenly found himself in the old world with its dusty accompaniments. The path by which he came out was not the way by which he had entered. In order to mark the entrance he planted a stake, and then the servant withdrew and disappeared.

The year following the master went again and tried to find the citadel of the genii, but there were only mountain peaks and impassable ravines, and where it was he never could discover.

As the years went by the master seemed to grow younger in spirit, and at last at the age of ninety he passed away without suffering. "When Chang was here on earth and I saw him for fifteen years," said the master, "I remember but one peculiarity about him, namely, that his face never grew older nor did his dirty clothing ever wear out. He never changed his garb, and yet it never varied in appearance in all the fifteen years. This alone would have marked him as a strange being, but our fleshly eyes did not recognize it."

The Ocean Seal

The Monastery of the Ocean Seal is one of the most important centers of Buddhism in Korea. It is in the town of Hyup-ch'um and counts its inmates by the hundreds. Its archives are piled with woodblocks cut with Sanskrit characters and the whole place is redolent with the odor of Buddhist sanctity. But it is the name which piques our curiosity and demands an explanation. The "Ocean Seal" does not mean the amphibious animal whose pelt forms an article of commerce but it means the seal with which a legal document is stamped.

Hong Sang-won was one of those literary flowers that are born to blush unseen and waste their sweetness on the desert air of central Korea. Virtue is its own reward but that reward seldom takes the form of bread and butter; so while Hong was virtuous he was lamentably poor. His literary attainments forbade his earning his living by the sweat of his brow so he earned it by the sweat of his slave's brow who went about begging food from the neighbors. Curiously enough this did not sully his honor as work would have done.

As he was sitting one day in his room meditating upon the partiality of fortune, a strange dog came running into the yard and curled up in a corner as if this had always been its home. It attached itself to Hong and accompanied him wherever he went. Hong took a great liking to the animal and would share with it even his scanty bowl of rice, much to the disgust of the faithful slave by whose efforts alone the food had been obtained.

One morning the dog began wagging its tail and jumping about as if begging its master to take a walk. Hong complied and the dog led straight toward the river. It ran into the water and then came back and seemed to invite its master to mount its back and ride into the stream. Hong drew the line at such a prank but when he saw the dog dash into the water and cross with incredible speed he caught the spirit of the occasion and so far curtailed his *yang ban* dignity as to seat himself on the dog's back. To his consternation the dog sank with him to the bottom of the river, but as he found no difficulty in breathing and naturally felt some delicacy about trusting himself alone to the novel element, he held fast to the dog and was rewarded shortly by a sight of the palace of His Majesty the Dragon King of the Deep. Dismounting at the door he joined the crowd of tortoises and octopi and other courtiers of the deep who were seeking audience

with their dread sovereign. No one challenged his entrance and soon he stood in the presence. The king greeted him cordially and asked him why he had delayed so long in coming. Hong carried on the polite fiction by answering that he had been very delinquent in paying his respects so late but that several species of important "business" had prevented his coming sooner. The upshot of the matter was that the sea king made him tutor to the crown prince, who studied his characters with such assiduity that in six months his education was complete.

By this time Hong was beginning to long for a breath of fresh air and made bold to intimate as much to His Majesty, who made no objection but insisted upon loading him down with gifts. The crown prince drew him aside and whispered:

"If he asks you to name the thing you would like best as a reminder of your stay with us, don't fail to name that wooden seal on the table over yonder." It was an ordinary looking thing and Hong wondered of what use it could be to him, but he had seen too many queer things to be skeptical; so when the king asked him what he would like he asked only for the wooden seal. The king not only gave him the seal but the more costly gifts as well.

With his capacious sleeve full of pink coral mixed with lustrous pearls and with the seal in his hand he mounted the dog and sped away homeward. A short half hour sufficed to land him on the bank of the stream where he had entered it, and with the dog at his heels he wended his way across the fields toward his former home.

When he arrived at the spot where his little thatched hut should be standing he found the site occupied by a beautiful and capacious building. Had he indeed lost the only place he could call home? Anxiously he entered the place and inquired for the owner. The young man who seemed to be in charge answered gravely that some twenty years before the owner had wandered away with his dog and never returned.

"And who then are you?" asked the astonished Hong.

"I am his son." Hong gazed at him critically and, sure enough, the young man looked just as his son would have looked. He made himself known and great was the rejoicing in that house. There were a thousand questions to be asked and answered,

"And where did this fine house come from?"

"Why, you see, the dog that you went away with came back regularly every month bringing in his mouth a bar of gold and then disappeared again. We soon had enough to build this place and buy all the surrounding rice fields."

"And it has been twenty years! I thought only six months had passed. They evidently live very fast down there under the sea."

Hong found no difficulty in adapting himself to the new situation. He was well on in years now but was very well preserved, as one might expcct from his having been in brine for the last twenty years. But he found no use for the seal that he had brought.

After several months had passed a monk came wandering by and stopped to talk with the old gentleman. In the course of the conversation it transpired that Hong had visited the Sea King's domain. The monk asked eagerly:

"And did you see the wonderful seal?"

"See it?" said Hong, "I not only saw it but I brought it back with me." The monk trembled with excitement.

"Bring it here," he begged.

Hong brought out the seal and placed it in the hands of the holy man. The monk took a piece of paper and wrote on it. "Ten ounces of gold." Then without inking the seal he pressed it on the paper and lo! it left a bright red impress without even being wet. This done, the monk folded the paper and setting fire to it, tossed it into the air. It burned as it fell and at the point where the charred remnants touched the ground was seen a bright bar of gold of ten ounces weight. This then was the secret. No matter what sum was asked for, the impress of that seal would surely bring it.

They kept it going pretty constantly for the next few days as you may easily imagine. The monk received an enormous sum with which he built the magnificent monastery and named it appropriately the Ha-in-sa, meaning "Ocean Seal Monastery."

He went all the way to India to bring the sacred Sanskrit books and the woodblocks were cut and piled in the library of the monastery. Beneath them was hidden the marvelous seal, but Koreans say that during the last Japan–China war it disappeared. The man who holds it is probably ignorant of its value. If his eye happens to fall upon this and he discovers the virtues of the seal we trust he will do the proper thing as Hong did by the monk who showed him its secret.

Yun Se-Pyong, the Wizard

Yun Se-Pyong was a military man who rose to the rank of minister in the days of King Choong-jong. It seems that Yun learned the doctrine of magic from a passing stranger, whom he met on his way to Peking in company with the envoy. When at home he lived in a separate house, quite apart from the other members of his family. He was a man so greatly feared that even his wife and children dared not approach him. What he did in secret no one seemed to know. In winter he was seen to put iron cleats under each arm and to change them frequently, and when they were put off they seemed to be red-hot.

At the same time there was a magician in Korea called Chon U-chi, who used to go about Seoul plying his craft. So skillful was he that he could even simulate the form of the master of a house and go freely into the women's quarters. On this account he was greatly feared and detested. Yun heard of him on more than one occasion, and determined to rid the earth of him. Chon heard also of Yun and gave him a wide berth, never appearing in his presence. He used frequently to say, "I am a magician only; Yun is a God."

On a certain day Chon informed his wife that Yun would come that afternoon and try to kill him, "And so," said he, "I shall change my shape in order to escape his clutches. If anyone comes asking for me just say that I am not at home." He then metamorphosed himself into a beetle, and crawled under a crock that stood overturned in the courtyard.

When evening began to fall a young woman came to Chon's house, a very beautiful woman too, and asked, "Is the master Chon at home?"

The wife replied, "He has just gone out."

The woman laughingly said, "Master Chon and I have been special friends for a long time, and I have an appointment with him today. Please say to him that I have come."

Chon's wife, seeing a pretty woman come thus, and ask in such a familiar way for her husband, flew into a rage and said, "The rascal has evidently a second wife that he has never told me of. What he said just now is all false," so she went out in a fury, and with a club smashed the crock. When the crock was broken there was the beetle underneath it. Then the woman who had called suddenly changed into a bee, and flew at and stung the beetle. Chon, metamorphosed into his accustomed form, fell over and died, and the bee flew away.

Yun lived at his own house as usual, when suddenly he broke down one day in a fit of tears. The members of his family in alarm asked the reason.

He replied, "My sister living in Cheolla Province has just at this moment died." He then called his servants, and had them prepare funeral supplies, saying, "They are poor where she lives, and so I must help them."

He wrote a letter, and after sealing it, said to one of his attendants, "If you go just outside the gate you will meet a man wearing a horsehair cap and a soldier's uniform. Call him in. He is standing there ready to be summoned."

He was called in, and sure enough he was a *kon-yun-no* (servant of the gods). He came in and at once prostrated himself before Yun. Yun said, "My sister has just now died in such a place in Cheolla Province. Take this letter and go at once. I shall expect you back tonight with the answer. The matter is of such great importance that if you do not bring it as I order, and within the time appointed, I shall have you punished."

He replied, "I shall be in time, be not anxious."

Yun then gave him the letter and the bundle, and he went outside the main gateway and disappeared.

Before dark he returned with the answer. The letter read: "She died at such an hour today and we were in straits as to what to do, when your letter came with the supplies, just as though we had seen each other. Wonderful it is!" The man who brought the answer immediately went out and disappeared. The house of mourning is situated over ten days' journey from Seoul, but he returned ere sunset, in the space of two or three hours.

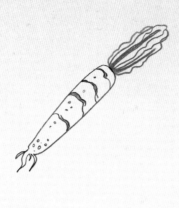

Old Timber Top

The fairies in the Korean province of Gangwon, which means River Meadow, were having great fun, when one of their number told how they played a trick on an ox-driver whom they called Old Timber Top. How he got such a strange name this story will tell.

This driver was a rich and stingy fellow who had made a fortune in lumber. He used to buy up all the trees he could. Then he would have them cut down and sawed up into logs and boards. His men would haul them away in their rough carts, drawn by stout bulls, to his lumber yard. In wintertime sleds were used, but whether it was the season of snow and ice, or of tree blossoms and flowers, the animal used to draw sleds or carts was always a bull.

You can see these patient carriers loaded with brushwood or sticks piled so high they seem to be carrying small mountains of twigs, grass and leaves for kindling, or with heavy logs of wood for fuel. Yet when the bull is very young, a mere baby, he has a happier time than a colt or little donkey, for he lives in the house and is the children's pet.

Old Timber Top sold his logs and boards at such high prices that the poor suffered. This was because they were cold and could not afford to pay so many strings of cash for fuel. The people used to say that the old fellow would skin a mosquito for his hide and tallow. So sometimes they gave him the nickname of Skin-flay.

Not many of the villagers were able to buy planks of wood thick and heavy and strong enough to keep their pigs from the tigers, which came down from the mountains and prowled about at night in the villages. These long-haired and black-striped beasts got to be so fond of pork, that even in the snow they would, without fearing the cold or the guns of the hunters, claw up the tops of the pens and get down among the squealing prey. They might get a baby pig at once or perhaps drag out and carry off enough of a big pork to feed their cubs for a week. All the stables and cow-houses had to be made very strong, for the tigers, when they had gone a good while without food, seemed to be hungry enough to eat a horse with all his harness on, and even a grown-up cow or ox. Yet as a rule, no tiger cared to taste either beef or horse meat, if he could get young pork or veal.

Old Timber Top was not satisfied to make money at his lumber yard only. It is the custom in Korea to plant the most beautiful trees around tombs or in the cemeteries. When this skinflint heard of a family which had become so poor that they must needs sell the splendid trees which had been planted around their ancestors' graves he sent his agents to buy the timber. These fellows would load up a horse with long ropes of copper and iron cash, coins that had a square hole in the middle and were strung together with twine made of twisted straw. It was a heavy horse load to carry twenty dollars' worth of coin. Arrived on the spot, after beating the owner down to the lowest price possible, Old Timber Top's men would go out, chop down and saw up the grand trees, leaving only the sawdust on the graves, while the people wept to lose what they loved.

In this way the landscape was spoiled and this made many villagers very angry at such a man, for the Koreans love natural scenery and almost worship fine trees, which had made the country beautiful for centuries.

But what cared Old Timber Top, provided he could pile up his strings of cash and jingle his silver?

In time, this hard old fellow could think of nothing else but how to get richer out of the wants and sufferings of other people. The wealthier he became, the more he wanted. Yet he did not get any happier. Nobody loved him, while many hated him.

At last he thought he would make a trip to Seoul, the great capital city. There he expected to receive honor and appointment to rank and office. Timber Top had a relative who was high in the king's service, who, he thought, would assist him.

To be an officer Timber Top knew would permit him even to wear a gorgeously shining mandarin's hat with wide flaps or wings on it and a long white silk coat with a big square on the breast of velvet or satin, embroidered with storks or dragons, clouds and waves. When he went out on the streets he could strut about, as if he were the lord of the universe; for he would then wear a hat so high and with such a round wide brim, that he would not dare to go out during a high wind, for fear of being blown away, like a ship in a tempest. In such a costume he would be saluted by servants and the common people, who would bow down before him, because they would think him a great man.

But how could he win such a position and gain the glory of it?

He was not a scholar, learned in books, or in law, or a doctor of medicine. Not being a soldier, either, he knew nothing of war. He could not ride on a monocycle, as a general did, drawn or pushed by four men and dressed in a long red coat studded all over with shining metal with a brass helmet on his head, on the top of which was a little dragon. He feared, even if he were appointed, he might fall off the one-wheeled vehicle and show what a fool he was.

Nevertheless this old fellow was so vain and full of conceit that he followed what was once the common custom in Korea. He took his journey to Seoul, leaving his family behind him to live on the cheapest kind of kimchi, with turnips and millet.

Now the Koreans are all famous for giving welcome and showing hospitality to their poor relations, and often they do this even to tramps and lazy people. When a man becomes rich or holds a high office, he usually has around him many hangers-on. Some, we should even say, were loafers.

So on arriving in Seoul, Old Timber Top took up his quarters in one part of his relative's big house. There he lived a long time and was treated decently, for he always was saying soft things and making flattering speeches to his host. In fact, he bowed down like a slave when in presence of his august master. Yet, in truth, he was despised even by the servants and work people.

In order not to wear his welcome entirely out he had to make from time to time a handsome present to his patron. This steadily reduced both his income and his fortune, and while these were shrinking his family at home suffered, so that, by and by, he received notice by letter that his business had dried up and soon no more money could be sent to him in Seoul. While he lingered news from home grew worse and worse. His wife was obliged to sell their house to pay debts. The next item was that she and her daughter were living in a wretched shanty at the end of the village and were no longer in society.

All this time those in Seoul who knew that the foolish fellow was as ambitious as ever to wear the fine white clothes of a scholar, or the gay colors of a soldier, declared that Old Timber Top had no brains. They even jested about a pumpkin set on shoulders, or they laughed when they declared that the wood, which he had sold so long, had gone to his head. They debated in the wine shops whether, if his skull were opened, pumpkin seeds or timber would be found inside of it.

So they, also, called him "Old Timber Top," meaning that inside his skull was a wooden head and no better than that of an idol carved out of persimmon wood, such as were so plentiful in the Buddhist temples. Others declared that he had a real head of bone and brains, but "he carried it under his armpits," as the saying was.

When the fairies heard all this, they unanimously resolved to reform the old fellow, even if they had to make an ox of him.

Timber Top, now poor and bankrupt, knew he must leave Seoul and go home and work for a living. When he made his final call on his rich Seoul relative and told him he must, to his great regret, take his leave and go back to his native village, he was not well received. Being too poor to buy a present to give to his host, on whose bounty he had lived so long, he was answered coldly and told to go and do as he liked.

And this, after years of fawning and gift-making! Not a word of thanks or appreciation! Poor Timber Top was down in the mouth and his heart was cold in his bosom. He knocked on his head with his fists, to find out whether, after all, it had really turned into timber.

On his way back, a big storm came on and when he came to a village inn, cold, wet and hungry, he begged for shelter overnight. The woman who kept it was the wife of a butcher, who was then away from home. This was an awful blow to Timber Top's pride, for butchers were held to be the lowest of people, and they were not even allowed to wear hats, like the rest of the men in Korea.

The woman was kind to the traveler. She gave him a hot supper and let him sleep in that room of the house which had the best stone floor, under which the flues from the kitchen fire ran. So he warmed himself and baked his clothes, which were sopping wet, until they were dry. He was so tired that he kept on sleeping till very late next morning, and nearly to the noon hour. He was altogether so comfortable that to him it seemed as if he were a great man in the capital, thus to receive such kind treatment.

Waking up from one of his naps, he heard what he thought was the big butcher, who had come home, asking of his wife in a gruff tone of voice, "Where is that ox? I must sell him this morning, for it is market day," he said.

In less than a minute more, the man and his wife entered the room with four sticks which the fairies had put there, a halter, and a rope, made of twisted rice straw, besides a thick iron ring, such as they put into bulls' noses, to make them obey their masters. Throwing down the iron ring and rope on the floor, in a trice they had thrust the stick under Old Timber Top's back. In a moment more, he felt horns growing out of his head, and his lips becoming thick as sausages. His mouth was as wide as a saucer and had big teeth growing on the upper jaw. A tail sprouted at his other end and the four sticks became four legs.

Before he could quite understand just what was going on, or what the matter could be, Old Timber Top was standing on four legs and the butcher was slipping the ring through his nose. Oh how it did hurt!

It was an awkward job to get the animal out of the room and through the narrow door, and some of the paper on the walls and the furniture suffered. But finally when out in the open air the bull, that was no other than what had been the man Timber Top, went quietly along to the marketplace. Any attempt to pull his head away, or to stop or run off, or in any way to misbehave, hurt his nose so dreadfully, that he quickly quit. The butcher needed to give only a slight jerk of the rope when the bull changed his gait and was as quiet as a lamb, even though as an animal he was big enough to gore the man and toss him on his horns, or crush him by trampling on him with his hoofs, if once he got angry.

One would have supposed that Timber Top would be a fighting bull, but no! In the marketplace he stood patiently and quietly for hours, hardly even stamping, when the flies began to bite.

"Oh that I had been as diligent and kept on at my honest occupation in my native village, as that fly!" mused the bull, that still had a man's memory.

At last there came a man with money to buy. He was a drover, who unloaded his pony and paid down many strings, or about twenty pounds, of copper and iron cash. The owner put the halter in the buyer's hand, and the new master then led off Timber Top to be sold to a butcher who lived up in his hometown in the north. This fellow intended first to fatten the animal and then turn him into steaks and stewing meat.

But on his way the new owner thought that, because he had made a good bargain, he must stop at a wine shop and have a drink. So he tied Timber Top's nose with the rope to the low wall, which enclosed a turnip field, and went inside the shop.

But while the drover's wine went in his wits went out, and he fell asleep and stayed in the shop a long time. In fact, it was as the old song said:

> *"First the man takes a dram,*
> *Then the dram takes another dram;*
> *Then the dram takes the man."*

Meanwhile Timber Top looked over the low wall, and, yielding to temptation, pulled up with his teeth some of the plants by the roots, first chewing the green leaves and then grinding the turnips and swallowing them.

Presto! The horns drew in and shriveled up. The ring dropped out of his nose and fell with a crash on the stones of the village path. His two forelegs turned into arms, the hair and hoofs became human legs and Old Timber Top was a man, and himself once again. To make sure of it he felt himself all over; pulled his own nose, felt around his back to see if he had a tail, and rubbed his head for horns. None there! He looked down and found he had only two legs. Then he swung his arms with delight, at being once more a man.

"Well named, Turn-up thou," he mused, "thou green plant with a mustard-like taste. Thou hast turned me inside out. Or, have the fairies been busy?"

He had hardly got these ideas through his half-wooden head, that he was on two legs and a man once more and could think like one, than he started on the road home. Just then the drover rushed out of the wine shop and accosted him, saying:

"Have you seen a stray bull anywhere near this place?"

Of course Timber Top using fine language, like a *yang ban*, said there was no bull in the neighborhood that he could see or knew of, and he had heard none bellowing. Then he gave the drover a look of contempt for being so stupid, and for asking of him, a gentleman, so foolish a question.

Yet after he was out of sight of the drover he slapped his thighs and went on joyfully. He kept on repeating to himself, "Sticks and turnips, turnips and sticks."

Then a big idea struck him, as if it were a tap on a wooden drum, such as one sees in Buddhist temples. It hit his brain so hard and so swelled his head, that his big Korean hat nearly toppled off. Immediately he put this idea into action.

He returned hastily to the inn and into the room in which he had been turned into a bull and stole the butcher's four fairy sticks, which stood in a corner, then he hurried at once over the roads towards the capital.

Reaching Seoul, he went to the house of his rich relative, where he had waited ten years for the fortune and the favor which did not come. Going into his host's bedroom, he tapped the high lord of the house with the fairy sticks, not hard, but only lightly.

Forthwith the man's head became horns at the top, with muzzle of thick lips in front. His hands turned into front hoofs and his legs into the hind quarters of a bull. Yet he was not entirely an ox, but only half animal and half man.

Old Timber Top stopped tapping and then went away, to await events, leaving the creature half man and half ox. He knew that soon he would be called in.

When the family of wife, many sons, several daughters, servants, retainers, hangers-on, and what not, saw their master half man and half ox, with horns and hoofs, they were distracted. Each one had his own notion of how to get him back into human form and like his former self. Each one ran all over town and into the adjoining villages to get and call in the *mudangs*.

These *mudangs* were the people, mostly women, whose business it was to drive out the imps and bad fairies, such as had, in this case, done the mischief. The kitchen maids stoutly declared that *tokkaebi* had wrought the change upon their master. They felt quite sure of it; but the men thought that the gods of the mountains were punishing him for his sins. On the other hand, the *mudang* woman said she would find out and get him back into his human skin, if they paid her enough money.

With drums and dancing and songs, screams, yells, and every sort of noise, the *mudangs* kept up such a terrible racket that it almost deafened the family. There were several of them called in, and they knew that they would all be well paid.

Meanwhile the doctors also kept on with their awful medicines, besides rubbing, pounding, blowing, and sticking needles into the bull and burning moxa, or little balls of cottony mugwort, on its hide.

Yet not a hoof or horn, not even a hair changed.

The *mudangs* declared that the imps had got inside the man and they must get them out. One fellow carried a big bottle to trap the imps and cork them in. Another insisted that they would have to use scissors and snip the skin in about a hundred places, thus making small holes to let the evil creatures out. Then they must bottle them up, lest they should get out and overrun the house and infest the whole town.

There seemed not so many chances of getting well as "one hair among nine oxen"; but the wife pleaded that they would put off using the scissors until all other means had failed. She did not want to see her dear husband's skin made into a colander, or sieve, if it could be helped.

At this point, when the din and the despair were worst and had come to a climax, Old Timber Top appeared. As some of the family had collapsed and lay helpless on the floor, and as all were too tired to ask questions, they at once made way for him. After looking at the patient with a face as wise as an owl's, Old Timber Top solemnly announced that only one thing could save him and that was a rare and wonderful drug, of which only he knew the secret, but which he could speedily procure. Of course the wife, sons and daughters instantly promised to give up their all, to see their husband and father himself again.

So while Timber Top went out to get the famous medicine, they all fell asleep, tired out, while the ox-man lay over on his side resting his horns and hoofs on the floor bed.

As for Old Timber Top, when once out on the street, he immediately began saying to himself, over and over again, "Turnips and sticks, sticks and turnips."

Going to a vegetable shop, he bought a fine large turnip, or turnip-radish, of the kind that grows in Korea, silvery white and about four feet long. He first peeled, then sliced, and finally pounded it into a sauce very fine. Then entering the house in triumph, he woke up the doctors, kicked the servants awake, and announced that the potent drug would soon restore their master. He solemnly bade them all watch and see him do it.

Pulling and hauling all together, five or six fellows were able to get the man-bull on his two hoofs and two feet and then Timber Top put a spoonful of the sauce on the big tongue.

At once a most marvelous change took place!

The horns shortened until they disappeared, the lips thinned, the mouth became smaller. Hoofs, hair, and hide departed into empty air. In the wagging of a dog's tail, the mighty man of the house had become himself again.

All the doctors, jugglers, and *mudangs* packed up their imp-bottles and medicines, and with their drums, flutes, bags, boxes and wares slunk away, while the family loaded Old Timber Top with grateful thanks and compliments.

As for the master, he declared Timber Top the greatest physician the world ever knew. He invited him to make the house his permanent home and showered upon him many gifts, with plenty to eat, and white clothes starched as white as snow. The hats with which he presented Timber Top were so big around and had a brim so wide, that he used them when covered with oiled paper covers as umbrellas in rainy weather, but he never went outdoors when the wind was blowing, for fear he would be whirled down the street. Besides this, he feared there was still much wood in his head, which might turn into a top and spin round, if he were not careful.

Old Timber Top set up a medicine office, practiced among the nobility and became physician to the king. When he visited the palace, he used a red visiting card, a foot long. He had a plastron, or square of velvet embroidery on his breast. He wore a string of amber beads as big as walnuts over his ears. He soon became fat with a double chin and plump fingers, showing that he reeked with prosperity. He lived to a good old age, his family were made comfortable, his sons and daughter married well, and he had seventeen grandchildren before he died.

Yet all the time, the fairies claimed that they did it all. They made the sticks work one way, and the turnips another, and they still play their tricks, especially on those with more or less wood in their heads.

An Aesculapian Episode

The boy was only five years old when his father died and left him heir to a large property, and by the time he was twelve his relatives had succeeded in absorbing the whole estate. Cast upon his own resources he wandered away in search of something to do to keep body and soul together. In course of time he came to the great salt works at Ulsan and hired himself out to one of the foremen there. Down beside the sea about on a level with tide water were scores of little thatched hovels. In each of them was a huge vat for holding salt water, with a fireplace beneath. Across the top of the vats heavy ropes were hung and these being dipped frequently in the boiling brine became covered with crystals of salt which were removed and sent to market. In one of these hovels our hero, Che-gal, was employed in bringing up sea water in buckets and in feeding the fires.

It was not long before his only suit of clothes became so saturated with salt that they formed a true barometer; for as salt attracts moisture, he could tell whenever it was going to rain, by the dampness of his clothes. When it was dry his clothes were always stiff with the dry salt.

One bright morning when everyone was putting out their rice in the sun to dry Che-gal begged his master not to do so as it was sure to rain. His master laughed at him but complied and in a short time a heavy rain came on that wet the other people's rice and caused a heavy loss. His master was astonished and asked Che-gal how he knew it was going to rain, but the boy kept his secret. In time everybody in that district found it well to wait for Che-gal's master to act before they would sow or reap their crops or put out their damp rice to dry. The boy's reputation spread throughout all the countryside and he was looked upon as a genuine prophet.

One day news came that the king had been attacked by a very mysterious malady which none of the court physicians could cure. Everything was done for him that human skill could do but still he sank. At last royal messengers came to Ulsan saying that the king had heard of Che-gal and wanted him to come up to Seoul and prescribe for him. The boy protested that he could do nothing, but they urged and commanded until he could do nothing but comply. When the road to Seoul had been half covered and the way led up the steeps of Bird Pass, three brothers intercepted the party and begged that the boy Che-gal turn aside to their house among the hills and prescribe for their mother who was at the point of death. The royal attendants protested but the three brothers carried sharper arguments than words; so the whole party turned aside and followed the brothers to their house, a magnificent building hidden among the hills.

What was Che-gal to do? He did not know the use of a single drug. To gain time he said that he could do nothing for the patient till the following morning. In the middle of the night he heard a voice outside the gate calling softly, "O, Mr. Hinge, Mr. Hinge." A voice from within replied and the visitors asked eagerly, "Can't we come in now?" The person addressed as "Mr. Hinge" replied in the negative and the visitors reluctantly departed. Now who could "Mr. Hinge" be? Che-gal had never heard such a queer name before; so he investigated. Going to the gate he called, "Mr. Hinge, Mr. Hinge."

"Well, what do you want?" came from one of the iron hinges of the door.

"Who was it that just called?" asked the boy.

"To tell the truth," answered the hinge, "the visitors were three white foxes masquerading as men. They have bewitched the old lady who is sick and came to kill her but I would not let them in."

"But you surely are not in league with these rogues. Tell me how I can save the old lady from them."

The Hinge complied and gave the boy explicit directions how to act upon the morrow, and at dawn the three brothers came to take his orders. He commanded that three large kettles of oil should be heated hot and that six men with three saws and six pairs of tongs should be secured. These things having been done he led the way down the path till he reached three aged oak trees standing by themselves. These he had the men saw off six feet from the ground. They all proved to be hollow. Then two men stood upon each stump and reaching down with the tongs lifted the kettles of hot oil and poured it down the hollow stumps. Two of the white foxes were scalded to death but the third one with nine tails leaped out and made its escape. When the party got back to the house the old lady appeared to be in articulo mortis but a good dose of ginseng tea brought her around and in an hour she was perfectly well.

The three brothers, and in fact the whole party including the royal attendants, were amazed and delighted with this exhibition of medical skill; and the brothers urged him to name his fee. He replied that the only thing he wanted was a certain old rusty hinge on one of the doors beside the gate. They expostulated with him but he firmly refused any other reward. The hinge was drawn out, and with this strange talisman safely in his pouch Che-gal fared gaily toward the capital, feeling sure that he held the key to the situation.

Late one afternoon he was ushered into the presence of his royal patient. He felt his pulse and examined the symptoms in a knowing way and then said that the next morning he would prescribe. At dead of night he took out the hinge and held a long consultation with it, the result of which was that in the morning he ordered six kettles of hot oil and five men with a *kara* or "power-shovel," as it might be called. Leading the way to a secluded spot behind the king's private apartments he ordered the men to dig at a certain point. Half an hour's work revealed a hole about eight inches in diameter. The oil was poured down this hole and to the consternation of all the witnesses the earth began to heave and fall above the spot and there emerged, struggling in his death agonies, an angleworm eight feet long and eight inches thick. When this loathsome object expired they all hurried in to the king who seemed to be breathing his last, but a good drink of ginseng soup brought him round again and he was entirely recovered. Che-gal said that the symptoms plainly pointed toward angleworm enchantment due to the fact that the worm had tasted of the king's bath-water.

Honors were heaped upon the young "physician" and he became the pet of the court. This might have finished his medical career had not news come from China that the Empress was the victim of some occult disease which defied the leeches of Peking, and the King of Korea was ordered to send his most distinguished physician to the Chinese court. Of course Dr. Che-gal was the one to go.

The rich cavalcade crossed the Yalu River and were half way across Manchuria when Che-gal felt the hinge stirring in his pouch. He took it out and had a consultation with it, in the course of which the hinge said:

"When you come to the next parting in the road make your whole company take the right-hand road and take the left yourself alone. Before you have gone far you will come to a little hut and call for a cup of wine. The old man in charge will offer you three bowls of a most offensive liquor but you must drink them down without hesitation and then ask as your reward his dog and his falcon."

The young man followed these queer directions but when the old man offered him the three bowls he found them filled with a whitish liquid streaked with blood. He knew the hinge must be obeyed, however, and so he gulped down the horrible mixture without stopping to think. No sooner was it down than the old man overwhelmed him with thanks and called him all sorts of good names. It appeared that the old man had been a spirit in Heaven but for some fault had been banished to earth and ordered to stay there till he could find someone to drink those three bowls of nauseating liquid. He had been waiting two hundred years for the chance which had now come and released him from his bondage. He offered Che-gal any gift he might wish but the young man refused everything except the dog and the falcon. These the old man readily gave and with dog at heel and bird on wrist the young practitioner fared on, meeting his cavalcade a few miles further along the road.

At last the gates of Peking loomed up in the distance and the young physician was led into the forbidden city by a brilliant escort. It was dusk as he entered and he was taken first to his apartments for some refreshment. Meanwhile the ailing Empress was suffering from intense excitement and demanding with screaming insistence that the physician from Korea should not be allowed to enter the palace but should be executed at once. Of course this was considered the raving of a disordered mind and was not listened to. The Empress declared that the Korean doctor should not come near her, but the following morning he was conducted to her apartment where he was separated from her only by a screen. Che-gal declared that if a string were tied about her wrist and passed through a hole in the screen he could diagnose the case by holding the other end. It was done but the Empress who seemed to be in the very extreme of terror fought against it with all her might. Che-gal held the string a moment as if some telepathic power were passing from the patient to himself, but only for a moment. Dropping the string he gave the screen a push which sent it crashing to the floor and at the same instant he rolled out from one of his flowing sleeves the little dog and from the other the hawk. The former flew at the Empress' throat and the latter at her eyes while the Emperor, who stood by, was struck dumb with amazement at this sort of treatment. A sort of free fight followed in which Emperors, Empresses, dogs and falcons were indiscriminately mixed, but the animals conquered and the Empress lay dead before them. The Emperor denounced Che-gal as a murderer but he stood perfectly still with folded arms and said only,

"Watch the body."

The Emperor turned to the corpse and to his horror saw it slowly change its form to that of an enormous white fox with nine tails. Then he knew the truth–that his Empress had been destroyed and this beast had assumed her shape.

"But where then is the Empress gone?" he cried.

"Take up the boards of the floor and see," the young man replied. It was done and there they found the bones of the unfortunate Empress, who had been devoured by the fox. Deep as was the Emperor's grief he knew that a heavy load had been lifted from the Middle Kingdom and he sent Che-gal back home loaded with honors and with wealth.

As he came to the Yalu River he felt the hinge moving in his pouch and took it out. The rusty bit of iron said, "Let me have a look at this beautiful river." Che-gal held it up with thumb and finger over the swift current of the stream and with one leap it wrenched itself from his hand and sank in the water. At the same moment a sort of mist came before Che-gal's eyes and from that hour he was blind. For a time he could not guess the enigma but at last it came to him. The hinge's work was done and it must go back to its own, but in order that Che-gal might not be called upon to exercise the physician's office again he was made blind.

So back to Seoul he went, where he lived till old age, an object of reverence to all the court and all the common people of Korea.

The Tenth Scion

L ong, long ago there existed a family of learned men, and there had been nine generations and in every one of them only one son. Each man had no sooner passed his examinations and taken his degree than he died. Thus the tenth generation had been reached, which again consisted only of one single representative. Now, when this tenth scion was ten years old, there came one day a monk to the house to beg alms. The mother sent her son to hand the alms to the monk. The latter looked the boy for a moment in the face and said: "Poor boy, thou art in a bad case." When the boy heard this, he ran to his mother and told her what the monk had said, and she at once sent a servant after the monk to recall him. Being asked the reason of his strange exclamation, the monk replied: "When the little monk looks into the boy's face, it seems to him that the child will be killed at the age of fifteen by a wild beast. Should he, however, escape the disaster, he will become a great man." The use of the first personal pronoun would be too presumptive a style of speech for a monk. The lady then inquired how the evil could be warded off. The monk replied: "It will be best to get the boy's traveling kit ready at once and to let him go wherever he likes." Whereupon the widows (mother, grandmother and great-grandmother), after embracing the boy and weeping bitterly, sent him away according to the monk's word.

As the boy did not know where to go, he simply wandered in this and that direction. Thus the time passed quickly, and in a twinkle his fifteenth year had arrived. One day he strayed from the main road and lost his bearings. He inquired of a passerby: "Will I be able to reach human dwellings if I go in this direction?" The man replied: "There are no human dwellings in these hills except a monastery. But a great calamity has befallen it, all the monks have died, and it stands empty now. Whoever enters its precincts is doomed to death." Innumerable times did the man try to dissuade him from going. But try as he would, the boy, having conceived the wish to go there by hook or by crook, set out for the monastery. When he reached it, he found it exactly as the man had told him: it was empty throughout. As it was winter just then and the weather very cold, he searched for charcoal and, when he had found some, made a blazing fire in a firebox. He then mounted with it to the garret above the Buddha image in the central hall and thus made himself invisible to any unforeseen caller. After the third watch (after 1 A.M.), there arose a great uproar. He peeped stealthily down and saw a crowd of animals enter. There was a tiger, a rabbit, a fox and a great many other animals. Each one took its place, and when they were all seated, the tiger addressed the rabbit: "Doctor Rabbit!" (The rabbit is thought by Koreans to be the learned one among the animals.) Receiving a ready response he continued: "Will the professor turn up a page of prophecy tonight and let us know whether we shall have success or failure?" The rabbit assented, pulled a small book from under the mat on which he was sitting, read in it and, after meditating a long while, announced his discovery: "Tonight the diagrams are strange." "How is that?" asked the tiger. "The prophecy runs as follows," replied the rabbit. "Sir Tiger will receive heaven-fire (heaven-fire is also equivalent to "great disaster") and Master Rabbit will meet with the loss of his goods." Scarcely had he said the words, when the boy threw a few live coals down on the tiger. This created such terror among the animals that they all took to flight.

The boy descended from the loft and, on looking about, found the little book out of which the rabbit had been reading. He picked it up and wondered whether he would after such a find meet with his predicted misfortune. He at once went outside the gate of the monastery, looked about in all directions, and noticed a light gleaming in a mountain-valley towards the east. Thinking there was a human dwelling there, he set out in that direction and found a one-roomed straw hut. When he called out for the master of the house, there appeared a maiden of sweet sixteen and welcomed him without any embarrassment. Thinking this a lucky circumstance, he entered the hut. He began to tell the girl about his past life. But as he was very tired, he lay down while the girl sat and did some needlework. Now, when she was threading her needle, she moistened her finger with her tongue, and he noticed to his horror that it was a black thread-like tongue (like a snake's). This discovery set him all a tremble, and he was thinking of running away, when the "thing," guessing his intention, said: "Although you escaped the former calamities, yet you shall not escape me. Before the bell in the monastery behind here rings three times you shall have become my food." Now, while the boy was inwardly sorrowing and expecting his death every minute, the bell rang all of a sudden three times. The girl had no sooner heard it than she threw herself at his feet and implored him for her life. He, pretending to possess immense power, shouted at her in the most imposing manner he could muster. The "thing" then drew a square gem from its side, offered it him and again pleaded with him for her life. He took the gem and asked what it was. She replied: "If you strike one corner and say: 'Money, come out!' money will appear. If you strike the second and say to a dead person: 'Live!' he will rise at once. By striking the third you can produce whatever you wish." As she stopped and did not give any explanation about the fourth corner, he asked her: "What does this corner effect?" When it seemed as though she was never going to tell him, he said to her: "Only if you tell me about this fourth corner will I let you go." Then as he insisted on getting an answer, she could no longer refuse and replied: "If you say to hateful people: 'Die!' they die." At once the boy pointed at her and cried: "Above all you are the most hateful to me. DIE!" Scarcely had he uttered the words, when a huge snake as thick as a pillar rolled at his feet and died.

This gave him such a fright that he left the house at once. As he was anxious to find out what could have made the bell ring so suddenly, he went back to the monastery and found a cock-pheasant with a stone in its beak lying dead in front of the bell. But what had this pheasant to do with him? As he tried to recollect the past, he remembered that when he was seven or eight years old he had one day gone with a servant up the hill near his house and found a cock-pheasant, which, being pursued by a hawk, had hid itself in the pine thicket. The servant had been for killing and eating the bird. But as he had cried with all his might and begged for it, the servant had, after warning him several times not to let it go, given it to him. He had taken it in his arms and admired it. The sheen of its feathers had been just dazzling, and he had thought it was altogether very beautiful to look at and would make a splendid toy. But then the pheasant had looked as though it were shedding tears, and out of pity he had let it fly. "Now," he said to himself, "without doubt, the pheasant has remembered that kindness, and when I was near dying, it saved me." Weeping bitterly the boy took off his waistcoat, wrapped the bird in it and buried it in a sunny spot.

In this way he had passed his fifteenth year and become sixteen years old, and it seemed to him that his fatal period was now ended. He therefore went to his native place and showed himself before his mother. You should have seen the fuss they made about him. His mother, grandmother and great-grandmother laughed and cried in turn. Their sobs shook them so that one would have thought it was a house of mourning. By and by the boy was married, had three sons and became, so they say, the founder of a great family.

The Home of
the Fairies

In the days of King In-jo (1623–1649) there was a student of Confucius who lived in Ga-pyong. He was still a young man and unmarried. His education had not been extensive, for he had read only a little in the way of history and literature. For some reason or other he left his home and went into Gangwon Province. Traveling on horseback, and with a servant, he reached a mountain, where he was overtaken by rain that wet him through. Mysteriously, from some unknown cause, his servant suddenly died, and the man, in fear and distress, drew the body to the side of the hill, where he left it and went on his way weeping. When he had gone but a short distance, the horse he rode fell under him and died also. Such was his plight: his servant dead, his horse dead, rain falling fast, and the road an unknown one. He did not know what to do or where to go, and reduced thus to walking, he broke down and cried. At this point there met him an old man with very wonderful eyes, and hair as white as snow. He asked the young man why he wept, and the reply was that his servant was dead, his horse was dead, that it was raining, and that he did not know the way. The patriarch, on hearing this, took pity on him, and lifting his staff, pointed, saying, "There is a house yonder, just beyond those pines, follow that stream and it will bring you to where there are people."

The young man looked as directed, and a *li* or so beyond he saw a clump of trees. He bowed, thanked the stranger, and started on his way. When he had gone a few paces he looked back, but the friend had disappeared. Greatly wondering, he went on toward the place indicated, and as he drew near he saw a grove of pines, huge trees they were, a whole forest of them. Bamboos appeared, too, in countless numbers, with a wide stream of water flowing by. Underneath the water there seemed to be a marble flooring like a great pavement, white and pure. As he went along he saw that the water was all of an even depth, such as one could cross easily. A mile or so farther on he saw a beautifully decorated house. The pillars and entrance approaches were perfect in form. He continued his way, wet as he was, carrying his thorn staff, and entered the gate and sat down to rest. It was paved, too, with marble, and smooth as polished glass. There were no chinks or creases in it, all was of one perfect surface. In the room was a marble table, and on it a copy of the Book of Changes; there was also a brazier of jade just in front. Incense was burning in it, and the fragrance filled the room. Beside these, nothing else was visible. The rain had ceased and all was quiet and clear, with no wind nor anything to disturb. The world of confusion seemed to have receded from him.

While he sat there, looking in astonishment, he suddenly heard the sound of footfalls from the rear of the building. Startled by it, he turned to see, when an old man appeared. He looked as though he might equal the turtle or the crane as to age, and was very dignified. He wore a green dress and carried a jade staff of nine sections. The appearance of the old man was such as to stun any inhabitant of the earth. He recognized him as the master of the place, and so he went forward and made a low obeisance.

The old man received him kindly, and said, "I am the master and have long waited for you." He took him by the hand and led him away. As they went along, the hills grew more and more enchanting, while the soft breezes and the light touched him with mystifying favor. Suddenly, as he looked the man was gone, so he went on by himself, and arrived soon at another palace built likewise of precious stones. It was a great hall, stretching on into the distance as far as the eye could see.

The young man had seen the Royal Palace frequently when in Seoul attending examinations, but compared with this, the Royal Palace was as a mud hut thatched with straw.

As he reached the gate a man in ceremonial robes received him and led him in. He passed two or three pavilions, and at last reached a special one and went up to the upper story. There, reclining at a table, he saw the ancient sage whom he had met before. Again he bowed.

This young man, brought up poorly in the country, was never accustomed to seeing or dealing with the great. In fear, he did not dare to lift his eyes. The ancient master, however, again welcomed him and asked him to be seated, saying, "This is not the dusty world that you are accustomed to, but the abode of the genii. I knew you were coming, and so was waiting to receive you." He turned and called, saying, "Bring something for the guest to eat."

In a little a servant brought a richly laden table. It was such fare as was never seen on earth, and there was abundance of it. The young man, hungry as he was, ate heartily of these strange viands. Then the dishes were carried away and the old man said, "I have a daughter who has arrived at a marriageable age, and I have been trying to find a son-in-law, but as yet have not succeeded. Your coming accords with this need. Live here, then, and become my son-in-law." The young man, not knowing what to think, bowed and was silent. Then the host turned and gave an order, saying, "Call in the children."

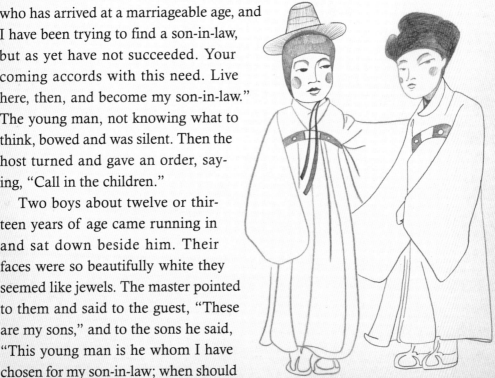

Two boys about twelve or thirteen years of age came running in and sat down beside him. Their faces were so beautifully white they seemed like jewels. The master pointed to them and said to the guest, "These are my sons," and to the sons he said, "This young man is he whom I have chosen for my son-in-law; when should we have the wedding? Choose you a lucky day and let me know."

The two boys reckoned over the days on their fingers, and then together said, "The day after tomorrow is a lucky day."

The old man, turning to the stranger, said, "That decides as to the wedding, and now you must wait in the guest chamber till the time arrives." He then gave a command to call so-and-so. In a little an official of the genii came forward, dressed in light and airy garments. His appearance and expression were very beautiful: a man, he seemed, of glad and happy mien.

The master said, "Show this young man the way to his apartments and treat him well till the time of the wedding."

The official then led the way, and the young man bowed as he left the room. When he had passed outside the gate, a red sedan chair was in waiting for him. He was asked to mount. Eight bearers bore him smoothly along. A mile or so distant they reached another palace, equally wonderful, with no speck or flaw of any kind to mar its beauty. In graceful groves of flowers and trees he descended to enter his pavilion. Beautiful garments were taken from jeweled boxes, and a perfumed bath was given him and a change made. Thus he laid aside his weath-er-beaten clothes and donned the vestments of the genii. The official remained as company for him till the appointed time.

When that day arrived other beautiful robes were brought, and again he bathed and changed. When he was dressed, he mounted the palanquin and rode to the Palace of the master, twenty or more officials accompanying. On arrival, a guide directed them to the special Palace Beautiful. Here he saw preparations for the wedding, and here he made his bow. This finished he moved as directed, further in. The tinkling sound of jade bells and the breath of sweet perfumes filled the air. Thus he made his entry into the inner quarters.

Many beautiful women were in waiting, all gorgeously appareled, like the women of the gods. Among these he imagined that he would meet the master's daughter. In a little, accompanied by a host of others, she came, shining in jewels and beautiful clothing so that she lighted up the palace. He took his stand before her, though her face was hidden from him by a fan of pearls. When he saw her at last, so beautiful was she that his eyes were dazzled. The other women, compared with her, were as the magpie to the phoenix. So bewildered was he that he dared not look up. The friend accompanying assisted him to bow and to go through the necessary forms. The ceremony was much the same as that observed among men. When it was over the young man went back to his bridegroom's chamber. There the embroidered curtains, the golden screens, the silken clothing, the jeweled floor, were such as no men of earth ever see.

On the second day his mother-in-law called him to her. Her age would be about thirty, and her face was like a freshly-blown lotus flower. Here a great feast was spread, with many guests invited. The accompaniments thereof in the way of music were sweeter than mortals ever dreamed of. When the feast was over, the women caught up their skirts, and, lifting their sleeves, danced together and sang in sweet accord. The sound of their singing caused even the clouds to stop and listen. When the day was over, and all had well dined, the feast broke up.

A young man, brought up in a country hut, had all of a sudden met the chief of the genii, and had become a sharer in his glory and the accompaniments of his life. His mind was dazed and his thoughts overcame him. Doubts were mixed with fears. He knew not what to do.

A sharer in the joys of the fairies he had actually become, and a year or so passed in such delight as no words can ever describe.

One day his wife said to him, "Would you like to enter into the inner enclosure and see as the fairies see?"

He replied, "Gladly would I."

She then led him into a special park where there were lovely walks, surrounded by green hills. As they advanced there were charming views, with springs of water and sparkling cascades. The scene grew gradually more entrancing, with jeweled flowers and scintillating spray, lovely birds and animals disporting themselves. A man once entering here would never again think of earth as a place to return to.

After seeing this he ascended the highest peak of all, which was like a tower of many stories. Before him lay a wide stretch of sea, with islands of the blessed standing out of the water, and long stretches of pleasant land in view. His wife showed them all to him, pointing out this and that. They seemed filled with golden palaces and surrounded with a halo of light. They were peopled with happy souls, some riding on cranes, some on the phoenix, some on the unicorn; some were sitting on the clouds, some sailing by on the wind, some walking on the air, some gliding gently up the streams, some descending from above, some ascending, some moving west, some north, some gathering in groups. Flutes and harps sounded sweetly. So many and so startling were the things seen that he could never tell the tale of them. After the day had passed they returned.

Thus was their joy unbroken, and when two years had gone by she bore him two sons.

Time moved on, when one day, unexpectedly, as he was seated with his wife, he began to cry and tears soiled his face. She asked in amazement for the cause of it. "I was thinking," said he, "of how a plain countryman living in poverty had thus become the son-in-law of the king of the genii. But in my home is my poor old mother, whom I have not seen for these years; I would so like to see her that my tears flow."

The wife laughed, and said, "Would you really like to see her? Then go, but do not cry." She told her father that her husband would like to go and see his mother. The master called him and gave his permission. The son thought, of course, that he would call many servants and send him in state, but not so. His wife gave him one little bundle and that was all, so he said goodbye to his father-in-law, whose parting word was, "Go now and see your mother, and in a little I shall call for you again."

He sent with him one servant, and so he passed out through the main gateway. There he saw a poor thin horse with a worn rag of a saddle on his back. He looked carefully and found that they were the dead horse and the dead servant, whom he had lost, restored to him. He gave a start, and asked, "How did you come here?"

The servant answered, "I was coming with you on the road when someone caught me away and brought me here. I did not know the reason, but I have been here for a long time."

The man, in great fear, fastened on his bundle and started on his journey. The genie servant brought up the rear, but after a short distance the world of wonder had become transformed into the old weary world again. Here it was with its fogs, and thorns, and precipice. He looked off toward the world of the genii, and it was but a dream. So overcome was he by his feelings that he broke down and cried.

The genie servant said to him when he saw him weeping, "You have been for several years in the abode of the immortals, but you have not yet attained thereto, for you have not yet forgotten the six things of earth: anger, sorrow, fear, ambition, hate and selfishness. If you once get rid of these there will be no tears for you." On hearing this he stopped his crying, wiped his cheeks, and asked pardon.

When he had gone a mile farther he found himself on the main road. The servant said to him, "You know the way from this point on, so I shall go back," and thus at last the young man reached his home.

He found there an exorcising ceremony in progress. Witches and spirit worshipers had been called and were saying their prayers. The family, seeing the young man come home thus, were all aghast. "It is his ghost," said they. However, they saw in a little that it was really he himself. The mother asked why he had not come home in all that time. She being a very violent woman in disposition, he did not dare to tell her the truth, so he made up something else. The day of his return was the anniversary of his supposed death, and so they had called the witches for a prayer ceremony. Here he opened the bundle that his wife had given him and found four suits of clothes, one for each season.

In about a year after his return home the mother, seeing him alone, made application for the daughter of one of the village literati. The man, being timid by nature and afraid of offending his mother, did not dare to refuse, and was therefore married; but there was no joy in it, and the two never looked at each other.

The young man had a friend whom he had known intimately from childhood. After his return the friend came to see him frequently, and they used to spend the nights talking together. In their talks the friend inquired why in all these years he had never come home. The young man then told him what had befallen him in the land of the genii, and how he had been there and had been married. The friend looked at him in wonder, for he seemed just as he had remembered him except in the matter of clothing. This he found on examination was of very strange material, neither grass cloth, silk nor cotton, but different from them all, and yet warm and comfortable. When spring came the spring clothes sufficed, when summer came those for summer, and for autumn and winter each special suit. They were never washed, and yet never became soiled; they never wore out, and always looked fresh and new. The friend was greatly astonished.

Some three years passed when one day there came once more a servant from the master of the genii, bringing his two sons. There were also letters, saying, "Next year the place where you dwell will be destroyed and all the people will become 'fish and meat' for the enemy, therefore follow this messenger and come, all of you."

He told his friend of this and showed him his two sons. The friend, when he saw these children that looked like silk and jade, confessed the matter to the mother also. She, too, gladly agreed, and so they sold out and had a great feast for all the people of the town, and then bade farewell. This was the year 1635. They left and were never heard of again.

The year following was the Manchu invasion, when the village where the young man had lived was all destroyed. To this day young and old in Ga-pyong tell this story.

The Trials of Two Heavenly Lovers

PRELUDE

Ching Yuh and Kyain Oo were stars attendant upon the Sun. They fell madly in love with each other, and, obtaining the royal permission, they were married. It was to them a most happy union, and having reached the consummation of their joys they lived only for one another, and sought only each other's company. They were continually in each other's embrace, and as the honeymoon bade fair to continue during the rest of their lives, rendering them unfit for the discharge of their duties, their master decided to punish them. He therefore banished them, one to the farthest edge of the eastern heavens, the other to the extreme opposite side of the great river that divides the heavenly plains (the Milky Way).

They were sent so far away that it required a full six months to make the journey, or a whole year to go and come. As they must be at their post at the annual inspection, they therefore could only hope to journey back and forth for the scant comfort of spending one short night in each other's company. Even should they violate their orders and risk punishment by returning sooner, they could only see each other from either bank of the broad river, which they could only hope to cross at the season when the great bridge is completed by the crows, who carry the materials for its construction upon their heads, as anyone may know, who cares to notice, how bald and worn are the heads of the crows during the seventh moon.

Naturally this fond couple are always heart-broken and discouraged at being so soon compelled to part after such a brief but long-deferred meeting, and 'tis not strange that their grief should manifest itself in weeping tears so copious that the whole earth beneath is deluged with rains.

This sad meeting occurs on the night of the seventh day of the seventh moon, unless prevented by some untoward circumstance, in which case the usual rainy season is withheld, and the parched earth then unites in lamentation with the fond lovers, whose increased trials so sadden their hearts that even the fountain of tears refuses to flow for their relief.

I.

You Tah Jung was a very wise official, and a remarkably good man. He could ill endure the corrupt practices of many of his associate officials, and becoming dissatisfied with life at court, he sought and obtained permission to retire from official life and go to the country. His marriage had fortunately been a happy one, hence he was the more content with the somewhat solitary life he now began to lead. His wife was peculiarly gifted, and they were in perfect sympathy with each other, so that they longed not for the society of others. They had one desire, however, that was ever before them and that could not be laid aside. They had no children; not even a daughter had been granted them.

As You Tah Jung superintended the cultivation of his estate, he felt that he would be wholly happy and content were it not for the lack of offspring. He gave himself up to the fascinating pastime of fishing, and took great delight in spending most of his time in the fields listening to the birds and absorbing wisdom, with peace and contentment, from nature. As spring brought the mating and budding season, however, he again got to brooding over his unfortunate condition. For as he was the last of an illustrious family, the line seemed likely to cease with his childless life. He knew of the displeasure his ancestors would experience, and that he would be unable to face them in paradise; while he would leave no one to bow before his grave and make offerings to his spirit. Again he bemoaned their condition with his poor wife, who begged him to avail himself of his prerogative and remove their reproach by marrying another wife. This he stoutly refused to do, as he would not risk ruining his now pleasant home by bringing another wife and the usual discord into it.

Instead of estranging them, their misfortune seemed but to bind this pair the closer together. They were very devout people, and they prayed to heaven continually for a son. One night the wife fell asleep while praying, and dreamed a remarkable dream. She fancied that she saw a commotion in the vicinity of the North Star, and presently a most beautiful boy came down to her, riding upon a wonderful fan made of white feathers. The boy came direct to her and made a low obeisance, upon which she asked him who he was and where he came from. He said: "I am the attendant of the great North Star, and because of a mistake I fell into he banished me to earth for a term of years, telling me to come to you and bring this fan, which will eventually be the means of saving your life and my own."

In the intensity of her joy she awoke, and found to her infinite sorrow that the beautiful vision was but a dream. She cherished it in her mind, however, and was transported with joy when a beautiful boy came to them with the succeeding springtide. The beauty of the child was the comment of the neighborhood, and everyone loved him. As he grew older it was noticed that the graces of his mind were even more remarkable than those of his person.

The next ten years were simply one unending period of blissful contentment in the happy country home. They called the boy Pang Noo (his family name being You, this made him You Pang Noo). His mother taught him his early lessons herself, but by the expiration of his first ten years he had grown far beyond her powers, and his brilliant mind even taxed his intelligent father in his attempts to keep pace with him.

About this time they learned of a wonderful teacher, a Mr. Nam Juh Oon, whose ability was of great repute. It was decided that the boy should be sent to this man to study, and great was the agitation and sorrow at home at thought of the separation. He was made ready, however, and with the benediction of father and caresses of mother, he started for his new teacher, bearing with him a wonderful feather fan which his father had given him, and which had descended from his great-grandfather. This he was to guard with special care, as, since his mother's remarkable dream, preceding his birth, it was believed that this old family relic, which bore such a likeness to the fan of the dream, was to prove a talisman to him, and by it evil was to be warded off, and good brought down upon him.

II.

Strange as it may seem, events very similar in nature to those just narrated were taking place in a neighboring district, where lived another exemplary man named Cho Sung Noo. He was a man of great rank, but was not in active service at present, simply because of ill-health induced by constant brooding over his ill fortune; for, like You Tah Jung, he was the last of an illustrious family, and had no offspring. He was so happily married, furthermore, that he had never taken a second wife, and would not do so.

About the time of the events just related concerning the You family, the wife of Cho, who had never neglected bowing to heaven and requesting a child, dreamed. She had gone to a hillside apart from the house, and sitting in the moonlight on a clean plat of ground, free from the litter of the domestic animals, she was gazing into the heavens, hoping to witness the meeting of Ching Yuh and Kyain Oo, and feeling sad at the thought of their fabled tribulations. While thus engaged she fell asleep, and while sleeping dreamed that the four winds were bearing to her a beautiful litter, supported upon five rich, soft clouds. In the chair reclined a beautiful little girl, far lovelier than any being she had ever dreamed of before, and the like of which is never seen in real life. The chair itself was made of gold and jade. As the procession drew nearer the dreamer exclaimed: "Who are you, my beautiful child?"

"Oh," replied the child, "I am glad you think me beautiful, for then, maybe, you will let me stay with you."

"I think I should like to have you very much, but you haven't yet answered my question."

"Well," she said, "I was an attendant upon the Queen of Heaven, but I have been very bad, though I meant no wrong, and I am banished to earth for a season; won't you let me live with you, please?"

"I shall be delighted, my child, for we have no children. But what did you do that the stars should banish you from their midst?"

"Well, I will tell you," she answered. "You see, when the annual union of Ching Yuh and Kyain Oo takes place, I hear them mourning because they can only see each other once a year, while mortal pairs have each other's company constantly. They never consider that while mortals have but eighty years of life at most, their lives are without limit, and they, therefore, have each other to a greater extent than do the mortals, whom they selfishly envy. In a spirit of mischief I determined to teach this unhappy couple a lesson; consequently, on the last seventh moon, seventh day, when the bridge was about completed and ready for the eager pair to cross heaven's river to each other's embrace, I drove the crows away, and ruined their bridge before they could reach each other. I did it for mischief, 'tis true, and did not count on the drought that would occur, but for my misconduct and the consequent suffering entailed on mortals, I am banished, and I trust you will take and care for me, kind lady."

When she had finished speaking, the winds began to blow around as though in preparation for departure with the chair, minus its occupant. Then the woman awoke and found it but a dream, though the winds were, indeed, blowing about her so as to cause her to feel quite chilly. The dream left a pleasant impression, and when, to their intense joy, a daughter was really born to them, the fond parents could scarcely be blamed for associating her somewhat with the vision of the ravishing dream.

The child was a marvel of beauty, and her development was rapid and perfect. The neighbors were so charmed with her, that some of them seemed to think she was really supernatural, and she was popularly known as the "divine maiden," before her first ten years were finished.

It was about the time of her tenth birthday that little Uhn Hah had the interesting encounter upon which her whole future was to hinge.

It happened in this way: One day she was riding along on her nurse's back, on her way to visit her grandmother. Coming to a nice shady spot they sat down by the roadside to rest. While they were sitting there, along came Pang Noo on his way to school. As Uhn Hah was still but a girl she was not veiled, and the lad was confronted with her matchless beauty, which seemed to intoxicate him. He could not pass by, neither could he find words to utter, but at last he bethought him of an expedient. Seeing some oranges in her lap, he stepped up and spoke politely to the nurse, saying, "I am You Pang Noo, a lad on my way to school, and I am very thirsty, won't you ask your little girl to let me have one of her oranges?" Uhn Hah was likewise smitten with the charms of the beautiful lad, and in her confusion she gave him two oranges. Pang Noo gallantly said, "I wish to give you something in return for your kindness, and if you will allow me I will write your name on this fan and present it to you."

Having obtained the name and permission, he wrote: "No girl was ever possessed of such incomparable graces as the beautiful Uhn Hah. I now betroth myself to her, and vow never to marry other so long as I live." He handed her the fan, and feasting his eyes on her beauty, they separated. The fan being closed, no one read the characters, and Uhn Hah carefully put it away for safe keeping without examining it sufficiently close to discover the written sentiment.

III.

Pang Noo went to school and worked steadily for three years. He learned amazingly fast, and did far more in three years than the brightest pupils usually do in ten. His noted teacher soon found that the boy could even lead him, and it became evident that further stay at the school was unnecessary. The boy also was very anxious to go and see his parents. At last he bade his teacher good-bye, to the sorrow of both, for their companionship had been very pleasant and profitable, and they had more than the usual attachment of teacher and pupil for each other. Pang Noo and his attendant journeyed leisurely to their home, where they were received with the greatest delight. His mother had not seen her son during his schooling, and even her fond pride was hardly prepared for the great improvement the boy had made, both in body and mind, since last she saw him. The father eventually asked to see the ancestral fan he had given him, and the boy had to confess that he had it not, giving as an excuse that he had lost it on the road. His father could not conceal his anger, and for some time their pleasure was marred by this unfortunate circumstance. Such a youth and an only son could not long remain unforgiven, however, and soon all was forgotten, and he enjoyed the fullest love of his parents and admiration of his friends as he quietly pursued his studies and recreation.

In this way he came down to his sixteenth year, the pride of the neighbor-hood. His quiet was remarked, but no one knew the secret cause, and how much of his apparent studious attention was devoted to the charming little maiden image that was framed in his mental vision. About this time a very great offi-cial from the neighborhood called upon his father, and after the usual formal-ities, announced that he had heard of the remarkable son You Tah Jung was the father of, and he had come to consult upon the advisability of uniting their families, as he himself had been blessed with a daughter who was beautiful and accomplished. You Tah Jung was delighted at the prospect of making such a fine alliance for his son, and gave his immediate consent, but to his dismay, his son objected so strenuously and withal so honorably that the proposition had to be declined as graciously as the rather awkward circumstances would allow. Both men being sensible, however, they but admired the boy the more, for the clever rascal had begged his father to postpone all matrimonial matters, as far as he was concerned, till he had been able to make a name for himself, and had secured rank, that he might merit such attention.

Pang Noo was soon to have an opportunity to distinguish himself. A great *gwageo* (civil-service examination) was to be held at the capital, and Pang Noo announced his intention of entering the lists and competing for civil rank. His father was glad, and in due time started him off in proper style. The examination was held in a great enclosure at the rear of the palace, where the King and his counselors sat in a pavilion upon a raised stage of masonry. The hundreds of men and youths from all parts of the country were seated upon the ground under large umbrellas. Pang Noo was given a subject, and soon finished his essay, after which he folded it up carefully and tossed the manuscript over a wall into an enclosure, where it was received and delivered to the board of examiners. These gentlemen, as well as His Majesty, were at once struck with the rare merit of the production, and made instant inquiry concerning the writer. Of course he was successful, and a herald soon announced that Pang, the son of You Tah Jung, had taken the highest honors. He was summoned before the King, who was pleased with the young man's brightness and wisdom. In addition to his own rank, his father was made governor of a province, and made haste to come to court and thank his sovereign for the double honor, and to congratulate his son.

Pang was given permission to go and bow at the tomb of his ancestors, in grateful acknowledgment for Heaven's blessings. Having done which, he went to pay his respects to his mother, who fairly worshiped her son now, if she had not done so before. During his absence the King had authorized the board of appointments to give him the high rank of *eosa*, for, though he was young, His Majesty thought one so wise and quick well fitted to travel in disguise and spy out the acts of evil officials, learn the condition of the people, and bring the corrupt and usurious to punishment. Pang Noo was amazed at his success, yet the position just suited him, for, aside from a desire to better the condition of his fellow men, he felt that in this position he would be apt to learn the whereabouts of his lady love, whose beautiful vision was ever before him. Donning a suitable disguise, therefore, he set out upon the business at hand with a light heart.

IV.

Uhn Hah during all this time had been progressing in a quiet way as a girl should, but she also was quite the wonder of her neighborhood. All this time she had had many, if not constant, dreams of the handsome youth she had met by the roadside. She had lived over the incident time and again, and many a time did she take down and gaze upon the beautiful fan, which, however, opened and closed in such a manner that, ordinarily, the characters were concealed. At last, however, she discovered them, and great was her surprise and delight at the message. She dwelt on it much, and finally concluded it was a heaven-arranged union, and as the lad had pledged his faith to her, she vowed she would be his, or never marry at all. This thought she nourished, longing to see Pang Noo, and wondering how she should ever find him, till she began to regard herself as really the wife of her lover.

About this time one of His Majesty's greatest generals, who had a reputation for bravery and cruelty as well, came to stop at his country holding nearby, and hearing of the remarkable girl, daughter of the retired, but very honorable, brother official, he made a call at the house of Mr. Cho, and explained that he was willing to betroth his son to Cho's daughter. The matter was considered at length, and Cho gave his willing consent. Upon the departure of the General, the father went to acquaint his daughter with her good fortune. Upon hearing it, she seemed struck dumb, and then began to weep and moan, as though some great calamity had befallen her. She could say nothing, nor bear to hear any more said of the matter. She could neither eat nor sleep, and the roses fled from her tear-bedewed cheeks. Her parents were dismayed, but wisely abstained from troubling her. Her mother, however, betimes lovingly coaxed her daughter to confide in her, but it was long before the girl could bring herself to disclose a secret so peculiar and apparently so unwomanly. The mother prevailed at last, and the whole story of the early infatuation eventually came forth. "He has pledged himself to me," she said, "he recognized me at sight as his heaven-sent bride, and I have pledged myself to him. I cannot marry another, and, should I never find him on earth, this fan shall be my husband till death liberates my spirit to join his in the skies." She enumerated his great charms of manner and person, and begged her mother not to press this other marriage upon her, but rather let her die, insisting, however, that should she die her mother must tell Pang Noo how true she had been to him.

The father was in a great dilemma. "Why did you not tell this to your mother before? Here the General has done me the honor to ask that our families be united, and I have consented. Now I must decline, and his anger will be so great that he will ruin me at the capital. And then, after all, this is but an absurd piece of childish foolishness. Your fine young man, had he half the graces you give him, would have been betrothed long before this."

"No! No!" she exclaimed, "he has pledged himself, and I know he is even now coming to me. He will not marry another, nor can I. Would you ask one woman to marry two men? Yet that is what you ask in this, for I am already the wife of Pang Noo in my heart. Kill me, if you will, but spare me this, I beg and entreat," and she writhed about on her cot, crying till the mat was saturated with her tears.

The parents loved her too well to withstand her pleadings, and resigning themselves to the inevitable persecution that must result, they dispatched a letter to the General declining his kind offer, in as unobjectionable a manner as possible. It had the result that was feared. The General, in a towering rage, sent soldiers to arrest Mr. Cho, but before he could go further, a messenger arrived from Seoul with dispatches summoning him to the Capitol immediately, as a rebellion had broken out on the borders. Before leaving, however, he instructed the local magistrate to imprison the man and not release him till he consented to the marriage. It chanced that the magistrate was an honest man and knew the General to be a very cruel, relentless warrior. He therefore listened to Cho's story, and believed the strange case. Furthermore, his love for the girl softened his heart, and he bade them to collect what they could and go to another province to live. Cho did so, with deep gratitude to the magistrate, while the latter wrote to the General that the prisoner had avoided arrest and fled to unknown parts, taking his family with him.

V.

Poor Pang Noo did his inspection work with a heavy heart as time wore on, and the personal object of his search was not attained. In the course of his travels he finally came to his uncle, the magistrate who had dismissed the Cho family. The uncle welcomed his popular nephew right warmly, but questioned him much as to the cause of his poor health and haggard looks, which so ill-became a man of his youth and prospects. At last the kind old man secured the secret with its whole story, and then it was his turn to be sad, for had he not just sent away the very person the *eosa* so much desired to see?

When Pang learned this his malady increased, and he declared he could do no more active service till this matter was cleared up. Consequently he sent a dispatch to court begging to be released, as he was in such poor health he could not properly discharge his arduous duties longer. His request was granted, and he journeyed to Seoul, hoping to find some trace of her who more and more seemed to absorb his every thought and ambition.

VI.

In the meantime the banished family, heart-sick and travel-worn, had settled temporarily in a distant hamlet, where the worn and discouraged parents were taken sick. Uhn Hah did all she could for them, but in spite of care and attention, in spite of prayers and tears, they passed on to join their ancestors. The poor girl beat her breast and tore her hair in an agony of despair. Alone in a strange country, with no money and no one to shield and support her, it seemed that she too must, perforce, give up. But her old nurse urged her to cheer up, and suggested their donning male attire, in which disguise they could safely journey to another place unmolested.

The idea seemed a good one, and it was adopted. They allowed their hair to fall down the back in a long braid, after the fashion of the unmarried men, and, putting on men's clothes, they had no trouble in passing unnoticed along the roads. After having gone but a short distance they found themselves near the capital of the province—the home of the Governor. While sitting under some trees by the roadside the Governor's procession passed by. The couple arose respectfully, but the Governor (it was Pang Noo's father), espying the peculiar feather fan, ordered one of the runners to seize the

women and bring them along. It was done; and when they arrived at the official yamen, he questioned the supposed man as to where he had secured that peculiar fan. "It is a family relic," replied Uhn Hah, to the intense amazement of the Governor, who pronounced the statement false, as the fan was a peculiar feature in his own family, and must be one that had descended from his own ancestors and been found or stolen by the present possessor.

However, the Governor offered to pay a good round sum for the fan. But Uhn Hah declared she would die rather than part with it, and the two women in disguise were locked up in prison. A man of clever speech was sent to interview them, and he offered them a considerable sum for the fan, which the servant urged Uhn Hah to take, as they were sadly in want.

After the man had departed in disgust, however, the girl upbraided her old nurse roundly for forsaking her in her time of trial. "My parents are dead," she said. "All I have to represent my husband is this fan that I carry in my bosom. Would you rob me of this? Never speak so again if you wish to retain my love"; and, weeping, she fell into the servant's arms, where, exhausted and overwrought nature asserting itself, sleep closed her eyes.

While sleeping she dreamed of a wonderful palace on high, where she saw a company of women, who pointed her to the blood-red reeds that lined the riverbank below, explaining that their tears had turned to blood during their long search for their lovers, and dropping on the reeds they were dyed blood-red. One of them prophesied, however, that Uhn Hah was to be given superhuman strength and powers, and that she would soon succeed in finding her lover, who was now a high official, and so true to her that he was sick because he could not find her. She awakened far more refreshed by the dream than by the nap, and was soon delighted by being dismissed. The Governor's steward took pity on the handsome "boy," and gave him a parting gift of wine and food to carry with them, as well as some cash to help them on, and, bidding him goodbye, the women announced their intention of traveling to a distant province.

VII.

Meanwhile Pang Noo had reached home, and was weary both in body and mind. The King offered him service at court, but he asked to be excused, and seemed to wish to hide himself and avoid meeting people. His father marveled much at this, and again urged the young man to marry; but this seemed only to aggravate his complaint. His uncle happened to come to his father's gubernatorial seat on a business errand, and in pity for the young man, explained the cause of the trouble to the father. He saw it all, and recalled the strange beauty of the lad who had risked his life for the possession of the fan, and as the uncle told the story of her excellent parentage, and the trouble and death that resulted from the refusal to marry, he saw through the whole strange train of circumstances, and marveled that heaven should have selected such an exemplary maiden for his son. And then, as he realized how nearly he had come to punishing her severely, for her persistent refusal to surrender the fan, and that, whereas, he might have retained her and united her to his son, he had sent her away unattended to wander alone; he heaped blame upon the son in no stinted manner for his lack of confidence in not telling his father his troubles. The attendants were carefully questioned concerning the conduct of the strange couple while in custody at the governor's yamen, and as to the probable direction they took in departure. The steward alone could give information. He was well rewarded for having shown them kindness, but his information cast a gloom upon the trio, for he said they had started for the district where civil war was in progress.

"You unnatural son," groaned the father. "What have you done? You secretly pledge yourself to this noble girl, and then, by your foolish silence, twice allow her to escape, while you came near being the cause of her death at the very hands of your father; and even now by your foolishness she is journeying to certain death. Oh, my son! we have not seen the last of this rash conduct; this noble woman's blood will be upon our hands, and you will bring your poor father to ruin and shame. Up! Stop your lovesick idling, and do something. Ask

His Majesty, with my consent, for military duty; go to the seat of war, and there find your wife or your honor."

The father's advice was just what was needed; the son could not, of necessity, disobey, nor did he wish to; but arming himself with the courage of a desperate resolve to save his sweetheart, whom he fancied already in danger from the rebels, he hurried to Seoul, and surprising his sovereign by his strange and ardent desire for military service, easily secured the favor, for the general in command was the same who had wished to marry his son to Uhn Hah; he was also an enemy to Pang Noo's father, and would like to see the only son of his enemy killed.

With apparently strange haste the expedition started off, and no time was lost on the long, hard march. Arriving near the seat of war, the road led by a mountain, where the black weather-worn stone was as bare as a wall, sloping down to the road. Fearing lest he was going to his death, the young commander had some characters cut high on the face of the rock, which read:

"Standing at the gate of war, I, You Pang Noo, humbly bow to Heaven's decree. Is it victory, or is it death? Heaven alone knows the issue. My only remaining desire is to behold the face of my lady Cho Gah." He put this inscription in this conspicuous place, with the hope that if she were in the district she would see it, and not only know he was true to her, but also that she might be able to ascertain his whereabouts and come to him. He met the rebels, and fought with a will, bringing victory to the royal arms. But soon their provisions gave out, and, though daily dispatches arrived, no rations were sent in answer to their constant demands. The soldiers sickened and died. Many more, driven mad by hardship and starvation, buried their troubles deep in the silent river, which their loyal spears had stained crimson with their enemies' blood.

You Pang Noo was about to retire against orders, when the rebels, emboldened by the weak condition of their adversaries, came in force, conquered and slew the remnant, and would have slain the commander but for the counsel of two of their number, who urged that he be imprisoned and held for ransom.

VIII.

Again fate had interfered to further separate the lovers, for, instead of continuing her journey, Uhn Hah had received news that induced her to start for Seoul.

While resting, on one occasion, they had some conversation with a passerby. He was from the capital, and stated that he had gone there from a place near Uhn Hah's childhood home as an attendant of the *eosa* You Pang Noo, who had taken sick at his uncle's, the magistrate, and had gone to Seoul, where he was excused from *eosa* duty and offered service at court. He knew not of the recent changes, but told his eager listener all he knew of Pang Noo's family.

The weary, footsore girl and her companion turned their faces toward the capital, hoping at last to be rewarded by finding the object of their search. That evening darkness overtook them before they had found shelter, and spying a light through the trees, they sought it out, and found a little hut occupied by an old man. He was reading a book, but laid it aside as they answered his invitation to enter, given in response to their knock. The usual salutations were exchanged, but instead of asking who the visitors were, where they lived, etc., etc., the old man called her by her true name, Cho Nang Jah. "I am not a Nang Jah" (a female appellation), she exclaimed; "I am a man!"

"Oh! I know you," laughed the old man; "you are Cho Nang Jah in very truth, and you are seeking your future husband in this disguise. But you are perfectly safe here."

"Ask me no questions," said he, as she was about to utter some surprised inquiries. "I have been waiting for you and expecting you. You are soon to do great things, for which I will prepare you. Never mind your hunger, but devour this pill; it will give you superhuman strength and courage." He gave her a pill of great size, which she ate, and then fell asleep on the floor. The old man went away, and soon the tired servant slept also. When they awoke it was bright morning, and the birds were singing in the trees above them, which were their only shelter, for the hut of the previous evening had disappeared entirely, as had also the old man. Concluding that the old man must be some heaven-sent messenger, she devoutly bowed herself in grateful acknowledgment of the gracious manifestation.

Journeying on, they soon came to a wayside inn kept by an old farmer, and here they procured food. While they were eating, a blind man was prophesying for the people. When he came to Uhn Hah he said: "This is a woman in disguise; she is seeking for her husband, who is fighting the rebels, and searching for her. He is now nearly dead; but he will not die, for she will rescue him." On hearing this she was delighted and sad at the same time, and explaining some of her history to the master of the house, he took her in with the women and treated her kindly. She was very anxious to be about her work, however, since heaven had apparently so clearly pointed it out to her, and, bidding the simple but kind friends goodbye, she started for the seat of war, where she arrived after a long, tedious, but uneventful tramp.

Almost the first thing she saw was the inscription on the rocks left by the very one she sought, and she cried bitterly at the thought that maybe she was too late. The servant cheered her up, however, by reciting the blind man's prophecy, and they went on their way till they came to a miserable little inn, where they secured lodging. After being there some time, Uhn Hah noticed that the inn-keeper's wife was very sad, and continually in tears. She therefore questioned her as to the cause of her grief. "I am mourning over the fate of the poor starved soldiers, killed by the neglect of someone at Seoul, and for the brave young officer, You Pang Noo, whom the rebels have carried away captive." At this Uhn Hah fainted away, and the nurse made such explanation as she could. Restoratives were applied, and she slowly recovered, when, on further questioning, it was found that the inn-people were slaves of You Pang Noo, and had followed him thus far. It was also learned that the absence of stores was generally believed to be due to the corrupt general-in-chief, who not only hated his gallant young officer, but was unwilling to let him achieve glory, so long as he could prevent it.

After consultation, and learning further of the matter, Uhn Hah wrote a letter explaining the condition of affairs, and dispatched it to Pang Noo's father by the innkeeper. The Governor was not at his country place, and the messenger had to go to Seoul, where, to his horror, he found that his old master was in prison, sent there by the influence of the corrupt General, his enemy, because his son had been accused of being a traitor, giving over the royal troops to the rebels, and escaping with them himself. The innkeeper, however, secured access to the prison, and delivered the letter to the unfortunate parent. Of course, nothing could be done, and again he blamed his son for his stupid secrecy in concealing his troubles from his father, and thus bringing ruin upon the family and injury to the young lady. However, he wrote a letter to the good uncle, relating the facts, and requesting him to find the girl, place her in his home, and care for her as tenderly as possible. He could do nothing more. The innkeeper delivered this letter to the uncle, and was then instructed to carry a litter and attendants to his home and bring back the young lady, attired in suitable garments. He did so as speedily as possible, though the journey was a long and tedious one.

Once installed in a comfortable home poor Uhn Hah became more and more lonely. She seemed to have nothing now to hope for, and the stagnation of idleness was more than she could endure. She fancied her lover in prison, and suffering, while she was in the midst of comfort and luxury. She could not endure the thought, and prevailed upon her benefactor to convey to His Majesty a petition praying that she be given a body of soldiers and be allowed to go and punish the rebels, reclaim the territory, and liberate her husband. The King marveled much at such a request, coming from one of her retiring, seclusive sex, and upon the advice of the wicked General, who was still in command, the petition was not granted. Still she persisted, and found other ways of reaching the throne, till the King, out of curiosity to see such a brave and loyal woman, bade her come before him.

When she entered the royal presence her beauty and dignity of carriage at once won attention and respectful admiration, so that her request was about to be granted, when the General suggested, as a last resort, that she first give some evidence of her strength and prowess before the national military reputation be entrusted to her keeping. It seemed a wise thought, and the King asked her what she could do to show that she was warranted in heading such a perilous expedition. She breathed a prayer to her departed parents for help, and remembering the strange promise of the old man who gave her the pill, she felt that she could do almost anything, and seizing a large weather-worn stone that stood in an ornamental rock basin in the court, she threw it over the enclosing wall as easily as two men would have lifted it from the ground. Then, taking the General's sword, she began slowly to manipulate it, increasing gradually, as though in keeping with hidden music, till the movement became so rapid that the sword seemed like one continuous ring of burning steel—now in the air, now about her own person, and, again, menacingly near the wicked General, who cowered in abject terror before the remarkable sight. His Majesty was completely captivated, and himself gave the orders for her expedition, raising her to relative rank, and giving her the choicest battalion of troops. In her own peculiarly dignified way she expressed her gratitude, and, bowing to the ground, went forth to execute her sovereign's commands, and attain her heart's desire.

Again donning male attire, she completed her preparations, and departed with eager delight to accomplish her mission. The troops having obtained an inkling of the strange character and almost supernatural power of their handsome, dashing leader, were filled with courage and eager for the fray. But to the dismay of all, they had no sooner arrived at the rebel infested country than severe rains began to fall, making it impossible to accomplish anything. This was explained, however, by the spirits of the departed soldiers, who appeared to the officers in dreams, and announced that as they had been sacrificed by the cruel General, who had intentionally withheld their rations, they would allow no success to the royal arms till their death was avenged by his death. This was dispatched to court, and believed by His Majesty, who had heard similar reports, oft repeated. He therefore confined the General in prison, and sent his son (the one who wished to marry Uhn Hah) to the front to be executed.

He was slain and his blood scattered to the winds. A feast was prepared for the spirits of the departed soldiers, and this sacrifice having been made, the storm ceased, the sun shone, and the royal troops met and completely vanquished the rebels, restoring peace to the troubled districts, but not obtaining the real object of the leaders' search. After much questioning, among the captives, a man was found who knew all about You Pang Noo, and where he was secreted. Upon the promise of pardon, he conducted a party who rescued the captive and brought him before their commander. Of course for a time the lovers could not recognize each other after the years that had elapsed since their first chance meeting.

You Pang Noo was given command and Uhn Hah modestly retired, adopted her proper dress, and was borne back to Seoul in a litter. The whole country rang with their praises. You Pang Noo was appointed governor of a province, and the father was reinstated in office, while the General who had caused the trouble was ignominiously put to death, and his whole family and his estates were confiscated.

As Cho Uhn Hah had no parents, His Majesty determined that she should have royal patronage, and decreed that their wedding should take place in the great hall where the members of the royal family are united in marriage. This was done with all the pomp and circumstance of a royal wedding, and no official stood so high in the estimation of the King, as the valiant, true-hearted You, while the virtues of his spouse were the subject of songs and ballads, and she was extolled as the model for the women of the country.

The Story of Ta-Hong

Minister Sim Heui-su was, when young, handsome as polished marble, and white as the snow, rarely and beautifully formed. When eight years of age he was already an adept at the character, and a wonder in the eyes of his people. The boy's nickname was Soondong (the godlike one). From the passing of his first examination, step by step he advanced, till at last he became First Minister of the land. When old he was honored as the most renowned of all ministers. At seventy he still held office, and one day, when occupied with the affairs of state, he suddenly said to those about him, "Today is my last on earth, and my farewell wishes to you all are that you may prosper and do bravely and well."

His associates replied in wonder, "Your Excellency is still strong and hearty, and able for many years of work; why do you speak so?"

Sim laughingly made answer, "Our span of life is fixed. Why should I not know? We cannot pass the predestined limit. Please feel no regret. Use all your efforts to serve His Majesty the King, and make grateful acknowledgment of his many favors."

Thus he exhorted them, and took his departure. Everyone wondered over this strange announcement. From that day on he returned no more, it being said that he was ailing.

There was at that time attached to the War Office a young secretary directly under Sim. Hearing that his master was ill, the young man went to pay his respects and to make inquiry. Sim called him into his private room, where all was quiet. Said he, "I am about to die, and this is a long farewell, so take good care of yourself, and do your part honorably."

The young man looked, and in Sim's eyes were tears. He said, "Your Excellency is still vigorous, and even though you are slightly ailing, there is surely no cause for anxiety. I am at a loss to understand your tears, and what you mean by saying that you are about to die. I would like to ask the reason."

Sim smiled and said, "I have never told any person, but since you ask and there is no longer cause for concealment, I shall tell you the whole story. When I was young certain things happened in my life that may make you smile.

"At about sixteen years of age I was said to be a handsome boy and fair to see. Once in Seoul, when a banquet was in progress and many dancing girls and other representatives of good cheer were called, I went too, with a half-dozen comrades, to see. There was among the dancing-girls a young woman whose face was very beautiful. She was not like an earthly person, but like some angelic being. Inquiring as to her name, some of those seated near said it was Ta-hong (Flower-bud).

"When all was over and the guests had separated, I went home, but I thought of Ta-hong's pretty face, and recalled her repeatedly, over and over; seemingly I could not forget her. Ten days or so later I was returning from my teacher's house along the main street, carrying my books under my arm, when I suddenly met a pretty girl, who was beautifully dressed and riding a handsome horse. She alighted just in front of me, and to my surprise, taking my hand, said, 'Are you not Sim Heui-su?'

"In my astonishment I looked at her and saw that it was Ta-hong. I said, 'Yes, but how do you know me?' I was not married then, nor had I my hair done up, and as there were many people in the street looking on I was very much ashamed. Flower-bud, with a look of gladness in her face, said to her pony-boy,

'I have something to see to just now; you return and say to the master that I shall be present at the banquet tomorrow.' Then we went aside into a neighboring house and sat down. She said, 'Did you not on such and such a day go to such and such a Minister's house and look on at the gathering?' I answered, 'Yes, I did.' 'I saw you,' said she, 'and to me your face was like a god's. I asked those present who you were, and they said your family name was Sim and your given-name Heui-su, and that your character and gifts were very superior. From that day on I longed to meet you, but as there was no possibility of this I could only think of you. Our meeting thus is surely of God's appointment.'

"I replied laughingly, 'I, too, felt just the same towards you.'

"Then Ta-hong said, 'We cannot meet here; let's go to my aunt's home in the next ward, where it's quiet, and talk there.' We went to the aunt's home. It was neat and clean and somewhat isolated, and apparently the aunt loved Flower-bud with all the devotion of a mother. From that day forth we plighted our troth together. Flower-bud had never had a lover; I was her first and only choice. She said, however, 'This plan of ours cannot be consummated today; let us separate for the present and make plans for our union in the future.' I asked her how we could do so, and she replied, 'I have sworn my soul to you, and it is decided forever, but you have your parents to think of, and you have not yet had a wife chosen, so there will be no chance of their advising you to have a second wife as my social standing would require for me. As I reflect upon your ability and chances for promotion, I see you are already a Minister of State. Let us separate just now, and I'll keep myself for you till the time when you win the first place at the Examination and have your three days of public rejoicing. Then we'll meet once more. Let us make a compact never to be broken. So then, until you have won your honors, do not think of me, please. Do not be anxious, either, lest I should be taken from you, for I have a plan by which to hide myself away in safety. Know that on the day when you win your honors we shall meet again.'

"On this we clasped hands and spoke our farewells as though we parted easily. Where she was going I did not ask, but simply came home with a distressed and burdened heart, feeling that I had lost everything. On my return I found that my parents, who had missed me, were in a terrible state of consternation, but so delighted were they at my safe return that they scarcely asked where I had been. I did not tell them either, but gave another excuse.

"At first I could not desist from thoughts of Ta-hong. After a long time only was I able to regain my composure. From that time forth with all my might I went at my lessons. Day and night I pegged away, not for the sake of the Examination, but for the sake of once more meeting her.

"In two years or so my parents appointed my marriage. I did not dare to refuse, had to accept, but had no heart in it, and no joy in their choice.

"My gift for study was very marked, and by diligence I grew to be superior to all my competitors. It was five years after my farewell to Ta-hong that I won my honors. I was still but a youngster, and all the world rejoiced in my success. But my joy was in the secret understanding that the time had come for me to meet Ta-hong. On the first day of my graduation honors I expected to meet her, but did not. The second day passed, but I saw nothing of her, and the third day was passing and no word had reached me. My heart was so disturbed that I found not the slightest joy in the honors of the occasion. Evening was falling, when my father said to me, 'I have a friend of my younger days, who now lives in Chang-eui ward, and you must go and call on him this evening before the three days are over,' and so, there being no help for it, I went to pay my call. As I was returning the sun had gone down and it was dark, and just as I was passing a high gateway, I heard the shrill whistle by which graduates command the presence of a new graduate. It was the home of an old Minister, a man whom I did not know, but he being a high noble there was nothing for me to do but to dismount and enter. Here I found the master himself, an old gentleman, who put me through my humble exercises, and then ordered me gently to come up and sit beside him. He talked to me very kindly, and entertained me with all sorts of refreshments. Then he lifted his glass and inquired, 'Would you like to meet a very beautiful person?' I did not know what he meant, and so asked, 'What beautiful person?' The old man said, 'The most beautiful in the world to you. She has long been a member of my household.' Then he ordered a servant to call her. When she came it was my lost Ta-hong. I was startled, delighted, surprised, and speechless almost. 'How do you come here?' I gasped.

"She laughed and said, 'Is this not within the three days of your public celebration, and according to the agreement by which we parted?'

"The old man said, 'She is a wonderful woman. Her thoughts are high and noble, and her history is quite unique. I will tell it to you. I am an old man of eighty, and my wife and I have had no children, but on a certain day this young girl came to us saying, "May I have the place of slave with you, to wait on you and do your bidding?"

"'In surprise I asked the reason for this strange request, and she said, "I am not running away from any master, so do not mistrust me."

"'Still, I did not wish to take her in, and told her so, but she begged so persuasively that I yielded and let her stay, appointed her work to do, and watched her behavior. She became a slave of her own accord, and simply lived to please us, preparing our meals during the day, and caring for our rooms for the night; responding to calls; ever ready to do our bidding; faithful beyond compare. We feeble old folks, often ill, found her a source of comfort and cheer unheard of, making life perfect peace and joy. Her needle, too, was exceedingly skillful, and according to the seasons she prepared all that we needed. Naturally we loved and pitied her more than I can say. My wife thought more of her than ever any mother did of a daughter. During the day she was always at hand, and at night she slept by her side. At one time I asked her quietly concerning her past history. She said she was originally the child of a freeman, but that her parents had died when she was very young, and, having no place to go to, an old woman of the village had taken her in and brought her up. "Being so young," said she, "I was safe from harm. At last I met a young master with whom I plighted a hundred years of troth, a beautiful boy, none was ever like him. I determined to meet him again, but only after he had won his honors in the arena. If I had remained at the home of the old mother I could not have kept myself safe, and preserved my honor; I would have been helpless; so I came here for safety and to serve you. It is a plan by which to hide myself for a year or so, and then when he wins I shall ask your leave to go."

"'I then asked who the person was with whom she had made this contract, and she told me your name. I am so old that I no longer think of taking wives and concubines, but she called herself my concubine so as to be safe, and thus the years have passed. We watched the Examination reports, but till this time your name was absent. Through it all she expressed not a single word of anxiety, but kept up heart saying that before long your name would appear. So confident was she that not a shadow of disappointment was in her face. This time on looking over the list I found your name, and told her. She heard it without any special manifestation of joy, saying she knew it would come. She also said, "When we parted I promised to meet him before the three days of public celebration were over, and now I must make good my promise." So she climbed to the upper pavilion to watch the public way. But this ward being somewhat remote she did not see you going by on the first day, nor on the second. This morning she went again, saying, "He will surely pass today"; and so it came about. She said, "He is coming; call him in."

"'I am an old man and have read much history, and have heard of many famous women. There are many examples of devotion that move the heart, but I never saw so faithful a life nor one so devoted to another. God taking note of this has brought all her purposes to pass. And now, not to let this moment of joy go by, you must stay with me tonight.'

"When I met Ta-hong I was most happy, especially as I heard of her years of faithfulness. As to the invitation I declined it, saying I could not think, even though we had so agreed, of taking away one who waited in attendance upon His Excellency. But the old man laughed, saying, 'She is not mine. I simply let her be called my concubine in name lest my nephews or some younger members of the clan should steal her away. She is first of all a faithful woman: I have not known her like before.'

"The old man then had the horse sent back and the servants, also a letter to my parents saying that I would stay the night. He ordered the servants to prepare a room, to put in beautiful screens and embroidered matting, to hang up lights and to decorate as for a bridegroom. Thus he celebrated our meeting.

"Next morning I bade goodbye, and went and told my parents all about my meeting with Ta-hong and what had happened. They gave consent that I should have her, and she was brought and made a member of our family, really my only wife.

"Her life and behavior being beyond that of the ordinary, in serving those above her and in helping those below, she fulfilled all the requirements of the ancient code. Her work, too, was faithfully done, and her gifts in the way of music and chess were most exceptional. I loved her as I never can tell.

"A little later I went as magistrate to Keumsan County in Cheolla Province, and Ta-hong went with me. We were there for two years. She declined our too frequent happy times together, saying that it interfered with efficiency and duty. One day, all unexpectedly, she came to me and requested that we should have a little quiet time, with no others present, as she had something special to tell me. I asked her what it was, and she said to me, 'I am going to die, for my span of life is finished; so let us be glad once more and forget all the sorrows of the world.' I wondered when I heard this. I could not think it true, and asked her how she could tell beforehand that she was going to die. She said, 'I know, there is no mistake about it.'

"In four or five days she fell ill, but not seriously, and yet a day or two later she died. She said to me when dying, 'Our life is ordered, God decides it all. While I lived I gave myself to you, and you most kindly responded in return. I have no regrets. As I die I ask only that my body be buried where it may rest by the side of my master when he passes away, so that when we meet in the regions beyond I shall be with you once again.' When she had so said she died.

"Her face was beautiful, not like the face of the dead, but like the face of the living. I was plunged into deepest grief, prepared her body with my own hands for burial. Our custom is that when a second wife dies she is not buried with the family, but I made some excuse and had her interred in our family site in the county of Ko-yang. I did so to carry out her wishes. When I came as far as Keum-chang on my sad journey, I wrote a verse—

'O beautiful Bud, of the beautiful Flower,
We bear thy form on the willow bier;
Whither has gone thy sweet perfumed soul?
The rains fall on us
To tell us of thy tears and of thy faithful way.'

"I wrote this as a love tribute to my faithful Ta-hong. After her death, whenever anything serious was to happen in my home, she always came to tell me beforehand, and never was there a mistake in her announcements. For several years it has continued thus, till a few days ago she appeared in a dream saying, 'Master, the time of your departure has come, and we are to meet again. I am now making ready for your glad reception.'

"For this reason I have bidden all my associates farewell. Last night she came once more and said to me, 'Tomorrow is your day.' We wept together in the dream as we met and talked. In the morning, when I awoke, marks of tears were still upon my cheeks. This is not because I fear to die, but because I have seen my Ta-hong. Now that you have asked me I have told you all. Tell it to no one." So Sim died, as was foretold, on the day following. Strange, indeed!

Hen versus Centipede

Song Ku-yun was a modest man, as well he might be, since he was only a *ye-rip-kun* or runner for one of the silk shops at Chong-no. His business it was to stand on the street and with persuasive tones, induce the passerby to change his mind and buy a bolt of silk rather than something else he had in mind. One day a slave woman came along and let him lead her into the silk shop. He did not expect he would get much of a percentage out of what such a woman would buy, but it would be better than nothing. When she had looked over the goods, however, she bought lavishly and paid in good hard cash. A few days later she came again and would listen to no other *ye-rip-kun* but Song, who felt much flattered. Again she bought heavily and Song began to hear the money jingle in his pouch. So it went on day after day until the other runners were green with envy. At last the slave woman said that her mistress would like to see him about some important purchases, and Song followed her to the eastern part of the city where they entered a fine large house. Song was ushered immediately into the presence of the mistress of the house, rather to his embarrassment; for, as we have said, Song was a modest man and this procedure was a little out of the ordinary for Korea. But the lady set him at his ease immediately by thanking him for having been of such help in making former purchases and by entering upon the details of others that she intended. Song had to spend all his time running between her house and the shops. One day the lady inquired about his home and prospects, and learning that he was a childless widower suggested that he occupy a part of her house so as to be more conveniently situated for the work she had for him. He gratefully accepted the offer and things kept going from bad to worse, or rather from good to better, until at last he married the woman and settled down to a life of comparative ease.

But his felicity was rudely shocked. One night as he was going homeward from Chong-no along the side of the sewer below "Hen Bridge," he heard his dead father's voice calling to him out of the air and saying, "Listen, my son, you must kill the woman though she is beautiful and seems good. Kill her as you would a reptile." Song stood still in mute astonishment. It was indeed his father's voice and it had told him to kill the good woman who had taken him out of his poverty and made him wealthy, who had been a kind and loving wife for more than a year. No, he could not kill her. It was absurd. The next night he passed the same way and again he heard the weird voice calling as if from a distance, "Kill her, Kill her like a reptile. Kill her before the seventeenth of the moon at dusk or you yourself will die." This gave Song a nervous chill. It was so horribly definite, the seventeenth at dusk. That was only ten days off. Well, he would think it over; but the more he thought about it the less possible it seemed, to take the life of his innocent wife. He put the thought away, and for some days shunned the place where, alone, the voice was heard.

On the night of the sixteenth he passed that way and this time the unearthly voice fairly screamed at him. "Why don't you do my bidding? I say, kill her or you will die tomorrow. Forget her goodness, look not upon her beauty. Kill her as you would a serpent; kill her—killkill." This time Song fairly made up his mind to obey the voice and he went home sad at heart because of the horrible crime that his father was driving him to. When, however, he entered the house and his wife greeted him, hung up his hat and brought his favorite pipe, his grim determination began to melt away and inside of an hour he had decided that, father or no father, he could not and would not destroy this woman. He was sure he would have to die for it, but why not? She had done everything for him and if one of them must die why should it not be he rather than his benefactress?

This generous thought stayed with him all the following day and when the afternoon shadows began to lengthen he made his way homeward with a stout heart. If he was to die at dusk he might as well do so decently at home. Everything was just as usual there. His wife was as kind and gentle as she always had been, and sudden death seemed the very last thing that could happen. As the fatal moment approached, however, his wife fell silent and then got up and moved to the farther side of the room and sat down in a dark corner. Song looked steadily at her. He was so fortified in his mind because of his entire honesty of purpose that no thought of fear troubled him. He looked at her steadily, and as he looked, that beautiful, mobile face began to change. The smile that always had been there turned to a demon's scowl. The fair features turned a sickly green. The eyes glared with the same wild light that shines in the tiger's eyes. She was not looking at him but away toward another corner of the room. She bent forward, her hands clutching at the air and her head working up and down and backward and forward as though she were struggling for breath. Every fiber of her frame was tense to the point of breaking and her whole being seemed enveloped and absorbed in some hateful and deadly atmosphere. The climax came and passed and Song saw his wife fall forward on her face with a shudder and a groan and lie there in a state of unconsciousness. But he never moved a muscle. He felt no premonition of death and he would simply wait until the queer drama was acted out to a finish. An hour passed and then he heard a long-drawn sigh, and his wife opened her eyes. The frenzy was all gone and all the other evil symptoms. She sat up and passed her hand across her brow as if to wipe away the memory of a dream. Then she came and sat down beside her husband and took his hand.

"Why did you not do as your father's voice ordered?" Song gave a violent start. How should she know? "Wh-what do you mean?" he stammered, but she only smiled gravely and said: "You heard your father's voice telling you to kill me but you would not do it; and now let me tell you what it all really means. You have acted rightly. Your own better nature prevailed and frustrated a most diabolical plot. That was not your father's voice at all but the voice of a wizard fowl that has been seeking my destruction for three hundred years. Don't look incredulous for I am telling you the truth. Now listen. For many a long century I was a centipede but after passing my thousandth year I attained the power to assume the human shape; but, as you know, the hen and the centipede are deadly enemies, and there was a cock that had lived nearly as long as I but who never had succeeded in killing me. At last I became a woman and then the only way to kill me was to induce some man to do it. This is why the cock assumed your father's voice and called to you and urged you to kill me. He knew that on this night at dusk he must have his last fight with me and he knew that he must lose. So he sought to make you kill me in advance. You refused and what you have just witnessed was my final conflict with him. I have won, and as my reward for winning I can now entirely cast off my former state and be simply a woman. Your faith and generosity have saved me. When you go to your office tomorrow morning go at an early hour, and as you pass the place where you heard the voice look down into the sewer and you shall see, if you need further evidence, that what I say is true."

Song assured her that he needed no further proof and yet when morning came he showed that curiosity is not a monopoly of the fairer sex by rising early and hurrying up the streets. He turned in at the Water Gauge Bridge and passed up alongside the sewer. He looked down, and there at the bottom lay an enormous white cock that had lived over four centuries but now had been vanquished. It was as large as a ten-year-old child and had it lived a few years longer it would have attained the power to assume human shape. Song shuddered to think how near he had come to killing his sweet wife, and from that day on he never ate chicken but he set his teeth into it with extraordinary zest.

Sources

The stories in this collection are taken from the following sources.

Korean Folk Tales: Imps, Ghosts and Fairies by Im Bang and Yi Ryuk, translated by James Gale (E. P. Dutton & Co., 1913)
Im Bang, born in 1640, was a disciple of the writer Song Si-yol. His writings have long been revered in Korea, and his reputation as a great scholar has endured for centuries. Yi Ryuk, who lived during the reign of King Sejo in the mid-15th century, was no less a scholar than Im Bang. The *Kuk-cho Inmul-chi* (Korea's Record of Famous Men) speaks of him as "a man of many offices and many distinctions in the way of literary excellence." Presbyterian minister James Gale arrived in Korea in 1888 to teach English and help translate the Bible into Korean. His books include *History of the Korean People* and a translation of *The Cloud Dream of the Nine*, the first work of Korean literature to be translated into English.

The Korea Review, edited by Homer Hulbert (Methodist Publishing House, Seoul)
Korea Review was a monthly magazine edited and largely written by the Congregationalist missionary Homer Hulbert between 1901 and 1906. Hulbert moved to Korea in 1886 after an education at Dartmouth College and Union Theological Seminary and spent the next two decades there preaching, teaching, writing, and pressing unsuccessfully for Korean independence during negotiations with Japan. As the stories in this collection demonstrate, ghosts and goblins numbered among his many interests.

Korean Fairy Tales by William Elliot Griffis (Thomas Y. Crowell Company, 1911)
The American minister and author William Elliot Griffis had a lifelong interest in East Asian culture and lived in Japan for several years in the 1870s. His numerous books include volumes of folklore from Europe, Japan and Korea as well as books on Korean and Japanese history.

Korean Tales by Horace Newton Allen (G. P. Putnam's Sons, 1889)
The American physician, missionary and diplomat Horace Newton Allen arrived

in Korea in 1884 to serve as doctor to foreign legations and the Korean royal family. In 1897 he was appointed U.S. ambassador to Korea, a position he held until 1905. He is the author of four books. He writes in the preface to *Korean Tales* that his motivation for writing that volume was to counteract the ignorance and stereotypes about Korea then commonplace in the West.

Other than *Korean Folk Tales*, the publications above rarely mention the Korean sources from which their material was translated or adapted. We thank the many unnamed Korean writers and storytellers who kept alive the tales in this book so that another generation can enjoy them.

Ten Thousand Devils
By Im Bang, from *Korean Folk Tales*

How Chin Outwitted the Devils
From *The Korea Review* vol. 3 (1903)

An Encounter with a Hobgoblin
By Im Bang, from *Korean Folk Tales*

The Great Stone Fire Eater
From *Korean Fairy Tales*

Cats and the Dead
From *The Korea Review* vol. 2 (1902)

The King of Hell
By Im Bang, from *Korean Folk Tales*

The Essence of Life
From *The Korea Review* vol. 2 (1902)

The Enchanted Wine Jug
From *Korean Tales*

The Swallow King's Rewards
From *Korean Tales*

The Story of Chang To-ryong
By Im Bang, from *Korean Folk Tales*

The Ocean Seal
From *The Korea Review* vol. 2 (1902)
Original title, "A Submarine Adventure"

Yun Se Pyong, the Wizard
By Im Bang, from *Korean Folk Tales*

Old Timber Top
From *Korean Fairy Tales*

An Aesculapian Episode
From *The Korea Review* vol. 2 (1902)

The Tenth Scion
From *The Korea Review* vol. 5 (1905)
Translated by Rev. G. Engel

The Home of the Fairies
By Im Bang, from *Korean Folk Tales*

The Trials of Two Heavenly Lovers
From *Korean Tales*

The Story of Ta-Hong
By Im Bang, from *Korean Folk Tales*

Hen Versus Centipede
From *The Korea Review* vol. 3 (1903)

"Books to Span the East and West"

Tuttle Publishing was founded in 1832 in the small New England town of Rutland, Vermont [USA]. Our core values remain as strong today as they were then—to publish best-in-class books which bring people together one page at a time. In 1948, we established a publishing outpost in Japan—and Tuttle is now a leader in publishing English-language books about the arts, languages and cultures of Asia. The world has become a much smaller place today and Asia's economic and cultural influence has grown. Yet the need for meaningful dialogue and information about this diverse region has never been greater. Over the past seven decades, Tuttle has published thousands of books on subjects ranging from martial arts and paper crafts to language learning and literature—and our talented authors, illustrators, designers and photographers have won many prestigious awards. We welcome you to explore the wealth of information available on Asia at www.tuttlepublishing.com.

Published by Tuttle Publishing, an imprint of Periplus Editions (HK) Ltd.

www.tuttlepublishing.com

Copyright © 2024 Periplus Editions (HK) Ltd.
Illustrations © Marco Furlotti
Consulting by Jaekeun & Tina Cho

Library of Congress Cataloging-in-Publication Data

ISBN 978-0-8048-5803-8

First edition
28 27 26 25 24
10 9 8 7 6 5 4 3 2 1   2411EP
Printed in China

TUTTLE PUBLISHING® is a registered trademark of Tuttle Publishing, a division of Periplus Editions (HK) Ltd.

Distributed by

North America, Latin America & Europe
Tuttle Publishing
364 Innovation Drive, North Clarendon
VT 05759-9436 U.S.A.
Tel: 1 (802) 773-8930
Fax: 1 (802) 773-6993
info@tuttlepublishing.com
www.tuttlepublishing.com

Japan
Tuttle Publishing
Yaekari Building 3rd Floor
5-4-12 Osaki Shinagawa-ku
Tokyo 141 0032
Tel: (81) 3 5437-0171
Fax: (81) 3 5437-0755
sales@tuttle.co.jp
www.tuttle.co.jp

Asia Pacific
Berkeley Books Pte. Ltd.
3 Kallang Sector #04-01
Singapore 349278
Tel: (65) 6741-2178
Fax: (65) 6741-2179
inquiries@periplus.com.sg
www.tuttlepublishing.com